ELEMENTAL MOON

THE ELDRITCH FILES
BOOK THREE

CALDWELLPRESS.COM

Published by Caldwell Press
Cover Design © 2014 by Lou Harper

Thank you for purchasing and reading Elemental Moon. It would be greatly appreciated if you could take a moment and leave an honest review of this episode within the guidelines of your favorite retailer.

QUALITY CONTROL: If you find typos or formatting problems, please contact ph8dra@comcast.net so they may be corrected.

If you want to be notified when Phaedra's next novel is released and get free stories and occasional other goodies, please sign up for her mailing list at her website, phaedraweldon dot com.

Your email address will never be shared and you can unsubscribe at any time.

As always, for my father. And for the readers.

The native hue of resolution
Is sicklied o'er with the pale cast of thought;
And enterprises of great pitch and moment,
With this regard, their currents turn awry,
And lose the name of action.

William Shakespeare, *Hamlet*

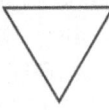

ONE

"You're kidding, right?" I gave my best friend and business partner my well-done *this-is-ridiculous* face, given our current situation. "Werewolves are *myths*."

Kyle Kendrick gave me his best version of the same face, which was visible in the flickering light of our waning fire. It was the beginning of January, just a few days into the new year. The moon overhead was full, which might account for the fact I could clearly see him as well as our other group member Ivan Westerfield, and my wolf familiar and mother, Grey.

Yes. That beautiful gray and white wolf is my mom. Deal. I had to.

After a two night drunkfest immediately following New Year's spent with my ex, I decided we, the Witches, needed to get back to the structure of ritual in our daily lives. So, I looked at a calendar and saw the full moon was coming up. Seemed like a great plan for us to center our energies and for me to get used to a whole new version of magic I wasn't happy with. Mom gave me a few pointers on full moon rituals, which were technically already written down in her Book of Shadows. But that book was at my Aunt Ina's house, a woman who wasn't really my aunt but a Vampire. And not just a plain Vampire, but a Leviathan Vampire. She wasn't there, having recently absconded with a soul whose body I had killed. I'd also just discovered the gardens of that house were full of dead bodies. Victims my so-called aunt had lured to her home, fed and then proceeded to go all *Hansel and Gretel* on.

While I was in high school.

Think this might be a lot to take in? You should see what it's like from my side of things. My name is Samantha Hawthorne. I'm a Witch, or I was a Witch, until the High Grand Master muckity-muck of the Witch's Parliament, or whatever they called themselves, decided I had something to do with the disappearance of a well-known Grimoire of sorts. A book known as the Malleus Maleficarum, or the Witch's Hammer. I call it the Hammer, cause the damn thing recently crushed my life.

I lost my connection to the Elements, something that made me who and what I was, but I'd gained an uncanny ability to use what is known as Arcane Magic. This is magic that has been forbidden for Witches to use for as long as I can remember. Most of the bad guys my group and I fight come from the realms where this magic thrives.

Including my ex…who might not be my ex…though I don't know.

Head spinning yet?

Good. Now pay attention.

"Guys," Ivan said as he moved in closer to us so we formed a three-backed triangle. I'm sure we looked pretty impressive. I had my hands out, my fingers laced with bright red smoky glitter. Ivan's hands were out in front, sparking with greenish electricity. And Kyle's hands, tattooed with two of the Elemental Symbols, glowed with bright yellow on his right for Air and brilliant blue on his left for Water. We were each ready to whammy anything that came at us. "Can we focus on the fact we're surrounded by a circle of really big wolves?"

He was right. Thus, the current situation I alluded to earlier.

The temperature was chilly, given it was January in Louisiana, and I could see our breath in the moonlight. Sometimes, but not this time, it dipped below freezing and made the news. I always wondered if the cause wasn't global warming related but Ceremonial Magician induced. They liked screwing up the weather. I wore my ex's leather jacket, 'cause mine had a hole in it and still reeked of Arcane taint.

Which had the aroma of two-day rotten chicken.

This jacket smelled like Detective Crwys Holliard. My ex. A fine piece of law enforcement who possessed the power of a flamethrower. Species? Unknown.

Grey sat at my side, panting, not even the least bit worried our full moon ritual had been interrupted by *lycanis humongous*. In fact, when I'd tried to talk to her, she'd abruptly said, *Sshh!* in my head.

The larger of the circle lumbered forward. I didn't know if that was the right word to use, but he didn't pounce, run or attack, so lumbered seemed right. His fur looked red in the moonlight, shadowed by darker hues of auburn and orange. His eyes glowed yellow as he approached—*me!*

Grey finally stood on all fours. I'd always thought of her as large. I obviously had no real appreciation of how big wolves could get. Next to Big Red there, mom looked like a puppy.

The two touched noses, then actually moved their heads as if to entwine their necks. I looked at Kyle, he looked at Ivan and Ivan looked at us.

"Is that normal?" Ivan whispered.

I lifted my shoulders in a shrug and finally prodded her thoughts again. *Mom? What is going on? Are they going to eat us?*

She finally answered me but there was something else in the thoughts…like an echo. *No, silly. They're here because they were drawn to your magic.*

Which magic? Ours combined or you mean my—

Your Arcane. They sensed it just before the new year and again after in these very woods. The last time it appeared, four days ago, two of their own vanished. When you activated yours tonight, they were drawn here. To you.

I gulped. *You did tell him that wasn't me, right? That I'm not responsible for missing wolves? And that you're my mom?*

He knows, Sam-Sam. Your Arcane doesn't have the same smell. And yes, he knows I'm your mother. I swear I heard an echo of laughter when she said that. *Her* laughter.

I relayed what she said to the other two.

Kyle's grin was infectious. "That's just so cool that you can talk to her like that."

It would be cooler if we weren't surrounded by wolves. All of them sat back on their haunches at once. Half of them panted with their tongues out and looked about as dangerous as a circle of puppies.

Really *BIG* puppies.

Everyone sat but Big Red. He continued to stand as mom turned to look at me. *You can put your weapons away.*

Oh. I lowered my hands and snuffed out the Arcane I'd powered up. Kyle clapped his hands and their lights extinguished. Ivan knelt down and pressed his hands to the ground, releasing the electricity into the earth. Once that was done we all turned to face Big Red.

Mom spoke to me. *The Aces wish to ask a task of you, by right of the Goddess Arduinna, to which all Lycans bow.*

That…was an epic line. I delivered it to the other two, though I was sure it didn't have the same impact as my mom's internal voice.

Ivan said, "Werewolves worship the moon?"

"Lycans. They prefer to be called Lycans," Kyle said. "The moon controls shifts between the apogee and the perigee."

Ivan and I *stared* at Kyle with wide eyes.

He looked back at us as if we'd each grown two heads. "What?"

"How do you know about apogee and perigee?" Ivan asked. "I had to Google that myself when you guys started talking about a full moon ritual. And how do you know what they prefer to be called?"

Mom cleared her throat in my mind. *Kyle has something he needs to tell both of you. But now's not the time.* When she said that, I didn't hear an echo. I assumed the echo meant she was sharing the thought, and for whatever reason she didn't want Kyle's secret shared. I felt I needed to answer the request so I looked at each of them and arched my brows in question. Do we help? Or do we get eaten?

When they both nodded, I turned back to mom and Big Red. "What is the task?"

Do you accept?

"Not until we hear the task. I don't want to promise them something I don't know if I can deliver."

Mom turned and looked up at Big Red who moved in front of me; his head nearly level with my own. Grey barked several times, but Big Red turned and gave her one hell of a roar. I jumped. So did she. It hurt watching mom take a few steps back, her ears down, whining like a wounded pup. So I started to call up a nice fireball to singe the big dog's ass off.

I wasn't prepared for what this bastard did next.

I froze as he stood up on his back legs, put his paws on my shoulders and bit into my shoulder. The whole action took less than a second. In my defense, I wasn't just standing there like some fragile deer waiting to be slaughtered. I had my mom's voice in my head saying, *Just be still. Don't move. Just be still.*

Naturally, I yelled out when he bit me. I assumed Kyle and Ivan moved or did something behind me because the wolves stood and growled low as they positioned themselves between us and the boys.

"What the hell?" Kyle called out. "You're gonna turn her into a Lycan!"

Uh. Whut?

The large wolf with his teeth buried into my shoulder blurred in front of me. The trees in the clearing spun around me as the wolf's warm fur was replaced by something softer, yet firmer. I stood with my head back, afraid to move because I didn't want my neck ripped out, and afraid to blast this son of a bitch into next year because my mom was in my head telling me everything was okay and I needed to relax. It was just a formality.

Getting bitten by a wolf was a formality?! Appetizer maybe, but...

Kyle whistled. Ivan swore.

Hands took my upper arms, just below my shoulders, and held me in a firm grip as Big Red pulled his teeth out and began licking the wound. I slowly became aware Big Red wasn't Big Red anymore. The wolf was gone, and in his place was a man. And the licking, though weird, made the pain go away.

When he stopped slobbering on my shoulder, he straightened. I looked up into the most handsome face I'd seen under a head full of red hair. The hair cascaded over his shoulders to his very bare nipples. A look down and I saw that Big Red the wolf was now Big Red the naked man.

I felt a full on body blush start from my forehead all the way to my feet. I was pretty sure if someone used a heat sensitive camera on me, I'd be flaming.

He put a very warm hand against my cheek. "*Trés belle, chérie.*" His voice was pure sex in a rich, Acadian accent. "Now *d'accord?*"

Oh my. "What...what did you just do?"

"He bit you," Kyle said from behind me. "Now you're going to become a Lycan."

"No," Big Red the naked man said. "She will not become my mate unless she breaks her promise."

"Promise?" I was getting my common sense back. Slowly. "What—I didn't make a promise. And what do you mean mate? I'm not your mate." I looked down at Grey standing beside Big Red, facing me. "What the hell? I said I wanted to hear the task first!"

I know. And I told him not to. But he thinks the best way for you to understand is to be a part of the pack. Temporarily, of course.

"Part of the pack?"

I caught a weird buzzing in my head and wasn't sure where it was coming from. Abruptly, my ears popped like they usually did in a plane and a crowd of voices filled the silence. I grabbed my ears at the volume and tried to block it out.

<Sister Mother Sorcière help attack us find them help us youhavetofindthem...thechildthechildthechild.>

The sheer number of voices in my head was deafening.

And then there was silence. I felt something move against my mind, brush against my soul as it inserted itself as a part of my consciousness. Big Red brushed up against me and pressed his very exposed body against mine as he put both of his hands against my face.

"I am Bastien Dante LeBlanc, Alpha of the Aces," he said as he moved one hand away from my face and gestured to the wolves around us. "And we want you to find our missing *frère*. Our brother. Our missing *soeur*. Our sister. And the *enfant de loup* she carries inside of her." He cast those yellow eyes down at me. "Or we will tear this city apart. *Sang pour le sang. D'accord, mon amie?*"

I didn't need my mom to translate for me, nor did I need the echo of their meaning in my head through the link the Alpha had just forced on me. They were desperate to find their pack mates, especially the wolf child their sister carried. And if they didn't find her alive, Mr. LeBlanc, the Alpha of an *actual* Werewolf pack, would declare war on the city of New Orleans.

Blood for blood.

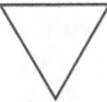

TWO

Standing outside after midnight on the bayou with a naked Alpha Werewolf insisting on blood for blood, was not how I had imagined my Wednesday night. The naked part wrecked my ability to find a place to look, and the just been bitten by a Werewolf part had my brain pinging around my skull like a ricochet bullet. I put my hand up to my shoulder to touch where he bit me. When my fingers came away with something dark and sticky, I was ready to bust heads.

Only I seemed to be rooted to the ground, and I desperately wanted someone to shut off all those voices!

At some point while I stood there in a stupor, Kyle had moved up to stand beside me, and he was talking.

"Mr. LeBlanc," Kyle said as he bowed just slightly. He also kept his eyes downcast. Screw that. I looked the big bastard in the eye. "I understand your pack's need to find your missing brethren, but I'm not sure if infecting our coven leader with your venom was necessary. Even if we find your people, how can you stop the change?"

I narrowed my eyes at Kyle. Why was he acting all customer service? I figured if anyone had a rude thing to say about Mister Well Hung it would be Kyle. I hadn't spent a lot of time around him since my warlocking and the utter obliteration of my dad's house, his body, his wife's body, and the body of their nurse.

Those were just the highlights of my December.

I knew from Crwys that Kyle had started dating Jack Roberts, one of the G-Men that invaded my magic shop and arrested Ivan last month on suspicion of cyber terrorism. Luckily, those charges were dismissed and that little cyber terrorism squad had moved on. Except for Jack, who seemed genuinely interested in Kyle. Given that most of Kyle's romances lasted the span of an afternoon, I'd call their three-week relationship a win.

But…was Kyle's relationship with Mr. Roberts actually making him turn a blind eye to a tall hot man's naked physique?

I put my hands to my head as Bastien answered and then shoved my fingers into my ears, anything to stop all that talking in the background.

"*Oui*, it was necessary. I can stop my gift after the fever begins. But like this, *ma petite* has choices to make. She will hear our family and know their urgency. Their sadness," he tilted his head as he lifted my chin with his index finger. "Children are precious to us because there are so few perigee born. So if you fail, then you will be my mate. With a *Sorcière*, we would be guaranteed another *enfant de loup* to replace the one we lose."

Wait a minute. Did he just say I'd have his baby?

Oh no, no, no, no…I pulled back from him, and that took a lot of will. Whatever he'd done to me, sunk into me…settled inside of me, was strong. I could feel him there, just on the edge of my thoughts, something moving in and out of my peripheral vision. I did *not* like this.

The Arcane Magic inside of me wasn't too happy either. It didn't like being watched. And neither did I. So…for the first time since destroying my dad's house, the forbidden magic inside of me and I were in agreement.

"You bastard!" Ivan yelled out and came up on my other side. He and Bastien were roughly the same height, but not quite the same build. Ivan's Asian heritage kept him slim and wiry, where Bastien was a bit more broad-shouldered with defined muscles. But he wasn't an over pumped body builder lookalike, which was nice. He was perfectly proportioned for his size and height. Not too big, and not to small.

And why was I sizing him up like I was shopping?

I put my right hand out and pressed it against Ivan's chest. "Ivan, step back. I'll handle it."

"Handle it? You let him bite you!"

Now I turned my own very pissed off face at him. To my delight, Ivan's brows disappeared under his thick black hair and he shrugged. "Fine."

"This one should be kept on a leash."

With every bit of strength I had, I slapped that big red headed mother across the face. His head snapped to his right and I had my striking hand in his face, finger pointed up his nose. "You shut the hell up. You obviously don't have a freak'n idea how to ask for a favor, do you? Well for starters, you don't go around biting people, and infecting them, just so they'll do your bidding to avoid turning into a killing, snarling, sniveling monster."

Bastien had a hand to his face and I realized none of the other wolves had stepped up to defend him. Not a one. Was it because we were linked and they knew deep down my intended slap wouldn't do any real damage?

"You need to stop me changing right now!"

At first I thought he was going to get mad. I mean, I had just slapped him. He didn't seem to care his jewels were in knee-up distance. He lowered his hand, shook his head, and the expression he gave me was not good. "Can't do, *chérie*. For the antidote to work, you have to be in the fever," he grinned. "We have two days before it starts. So first we find our own."

I could hear their laughter in my head and I hated it. They knew they had me by the balls, so to speak. And since I didn't know what he'd use to stop his venom, I didn't know how to get around this intolerable situation. And that just made me madder. As their laughter intensified in my head, I could make out distinct voices now and then. There were cracks about my hair, my lack of a shape, my small tits and then finally about how I was too weak to bear a prince of the wolves.

I closed my eyes and thought about burning them all, lighting them on fire, destroying them where they sat, stood and laughed inside their heads. And once I had all of those destructive thoughts, I wrapped them in a nice package and blew it back out to them.

All of them. To every wolf linked to the pack mind.

Wolves jumped around us, whined and yelped out. Some rolled on the ground as I blasted their thoughts back at them.

Even Bastien looked in pain for a short minute or two, before he looked past me to his pack and then narrowed his yellow eyes at me. "You would dare?"

"You dared. I'm just letting you and your knuckleheads know that I am not your mate, that I will never bear you children and that I am in control of me," I turned and looked at the circle of rolling, writhing wolves. "Do I make myself clear?"

Oh dear… Grey said in a sad voice.

What? You think that was too much? They've got to know they can't just control people like that. Not me! I'm my own person!

13

She looked up at me and when I looked down at her said, *It's not that. It's...he* really *likes you now.*

Oh, damn.

When I heard all of them answer yes, I slammed the door shut. Just a simple visualization of a door in my mind slamming shut to their thoughts. I locked the door up tight and kept the key. Once that was done, I looked at Bastien. "I suggest you start talking so we can find your people."

Part of me didn't want to help him at all, but the larger part of me was thinking of the unborn child. Human or wolf, I couldn't turn my back on a baby.

Bastien straightened up and squared his shoulders. This just made him look like a strutting peacock to me. Yes, I was still pissed off.

"Five days ago, we were hunting in the bayou and smelled something wrong. With the foul scent came screams. We believed it was a non-pack wolf. *Mon frére* took off after the noise, followed by his den mate," Bastien looked around at the recovering wolves. "We gave chase, but they were gone. We caught the scent of their blood and followed it to the edge of the city to a morgue."

"So you know one of your brothers is dead."

"*Non. Mon frére* still lives. *Petite soeur* is gone. They are both missing. But the blood in the morgue is wolf and probably the source of the screams we heard, so we hope the body will give us a clue as to who harmed it and took our family."

I had to think about the usage of the language before I clarified. "Are you saying the brother that's missing is your actual blood brother? Familial kin."

"*Oui.*"

"And the female that's missing, the one that's pregnant, is your brother's mate?"

"*Oui.*"

Ivan spoke up, his voice a lot calmer. "Why can't you go get it yourself? If there's a body there, the NOPD would probably love to have someone ID it."

Bastien's face darkened. I feared for a second he might lunge after Ivan and that wasn't going to work for me. "Ivan, have you seen any mention of any unidentified bodies being found in the bayou recently?"

He shook his head.

"That's your answer. If Bastien or any of his pack goes straight to that morgue and requests to see a specific body, it'll look suspicious.

Then they'll ask questions the pack isn't prepared to answer. And," I held up my finger. "This wolf isn't part of their pack. They may not be able to ID it."

The edge of Bastien's sensuous mouth pulled up. "Smart."

Asshole.

"*D'accord?*" Bastien asked.

I looked at Ivan and Kyle.

Ivan made a face. "Do we have a choice? I personally don't want to see you end up as this lug's breeding mate."

Bastien growled.

I held my hand up in Bastien's face. "Down puppy. Kyle?"

Kyle's hesitation surprised me. I figured as my friend he'd be just as pissed off about the bite thing.

I leaned toward him. "Hello?"

"There's something you need to know before we do this."

"What? You're secretly a Werewolf?"

"No," he did this weird shrug by raising his shoulders all the way up to his ears and held out his hands. "But I'm dating one."

A movement behind Kyle caught my attention. Another human form stood up in the shadows. As this one stepped closer and into the dimming firelight, my jaw hit the floor.

Jack Roberts.

Ivan and I both looked at Kyle, but he was looking at Jack.

"*Mon dieu,*" Ivan said as he slapped his hands to his cheeks.

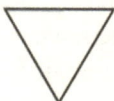

THREE

Now I'd seen everything. I looked back at Bastien, who didn't seem that surprised. "You knew they were dating?"

"There is nothing in Jack's mind I do not know."

Jack cleared his throat. He looked less comfortable with his own nakedness. "It's the link, Sam. The pack's known from the moment I set eyes on Kyle."

I...didn't know what to say. But this answered a few questions that had popped up tonight. Like how Kyle knew how to talk to an Alpha, and he knew they preferred to be called Lycans. It was because he'd been sleeping with one!

Fatigue crept up my back as I looked at the burning embers in our fire.

"Sam?" Kyle said. "Are you upset?"

"No. Why should I be upset? I've lost my dad, my Elementals, and now a Werewolf has bitten me as a threat so that I'll find his missing brother and his wife. What's to be upset about?"

"Uh..." Ivan said. Poor boy didn't know how to react to what I'd just said. "Sam, is there anything I can do—" Ivan leaned his head to his shoulder.

He was the sweetest guy. Cute too, with his Japanese American features. I didn't feel right about this task the wolves dumped on me. And I did not want to be this wolf's mate. The first person I planned on talking to was Crwys. Hopefully he'd heard something else on my warlocking. Like when it could be removed. The Hammer had been found, or rather a copy of it had been found. A copy I'd ask him to make. As to my copy? It was gone. Regardless of whether I had it or not, Parliament had their copy. I was innocent. But I was still warlocked.

16

I should be freed. But apparently their process on reversing their decisions moved at the speed of ice.

"You have a deal, Mr. LeBlanc. But with a few caveats."

Bastien smiled. "Please speak."

I could see my handprint on the side of his face, quite prominent in the moonlight. "One, you won't go looking for blood. Period. Whether we find your people or not."

"Done."

"And two, you have got to talk to me with clothes on and not in fur suits, got it?"

He laughed and looked down at Grey who'd been sitting there this whole time, very quietly. "*Ma petite*, paladin. She is as you said, fierce." He was in my space in seconds. He took my hand and brought it to his lips and pressed a kiss to the back of it. His skin was hot. So much like Crwys's temperature. "You have promises. I will wait on news," he kissed my hand again. "*Bonne nuit, chérie.*" And then he was gone and in his place was the musty scent of him.

Jack no longer stood as a naked man, but a large black wolf beside Kyle.

"*Jai faim!*" Bastien called out just before he blurred back into Big Red and the whole pack ran off into the foggy woods.

All four of us watched as they disappeared.

"Well, that's not something you see every day."

I elbowed Ivan and immediately focused my ire on Kyle. "You want to start talking now?"

But Kyle wasn't going to be bullied, especially not by me. He held up a finger and pointed to the low crackling embers, which was pretty much all that was left of our fire. "If we're going to have a full moon ritual, I suggest we get on with it. If not, I say we put the fire out, pack up and head back to the shop. Jack will meet us there when he's done."

"If it's all the same to you two," Ivan said as he shoved his hands into the pockets of his jacket. "I'm up for Kyle talking about his boyfriend being a wolf, and some hot chocolate made with real milk, rather than a ritual."

I hated to admit it, but I just wasn't in the mood to be real ritually. Or witchy. And hot chocolate sounded good.

Kyle put the fire out as Ivan and I gathered our things. Once back in my Jeep I pulled out my phone. No bars. "Anyone got service?"

"Nope," Kyle said as the light from his phone cast deep shadows across his face.

"Ivan?"

Ivan had his eyes closed and his hands out. I could see the eerie green glow of his magic as it ebbed and flowed around him. He waved his hands and dismissed it. "Nah. The web's too thin out here for me to connect without bouncing off it. Funny to think there are still vestiges of wilderness in this world, isn't it?"

I grinned at his reflection in my rear view mirror. Ivan's Gift, the power bestowed upon him by what we called the God Mother, was that he could touch the Cyber World. He could dive into Cyberspace and manipulate it with a thought. It was a new power—something I'd never seen before. But we'd recently learned he wasn't the only one of his kind.

Kyle was a Hedge Witch. This magic was considered more common; except for the fact Kyle was a man. Most Hedge Witches were female. A Hedge Witch worked with herbs and spells and could literally create magic from the spirits of organic items found around them.

And then there was me. I was an Elemental Witch and could, at one time, control the Elements with my Gift. I was also on my way to learning Spirit, the fifth Element. And this brings me back to the warlocking, where my Gift was taken from me. Usually warlocked Witches go insane with the stress caused by being unable to use their magic. Especially Elemental Witches. Our connection to the Elementals is personal, so taking them from us was like destroying our family.

And I'd already had enough of my family destroyed.

I was waiting for Parliament to give me back my Gift, but all I was getting was a recorded, "We'll get back to you on that," message. It was going on a month now and I was losing my patience.

"You don't mind if Jack comes to the shop, do you?"

So first he tells me Jack's coming, and now he's asking. I backed the Jeep out of the flat space I parked in and maneuvered it over some bumpy terrain to get back to the dirt road. "When?"

"Late tonight?"

"Sure." Once on the road I relaxed into my seat and smiled at Grey as she settled into the front passenger seat for the ride home. "As long as you'll strip down to your tighty-whiteys and show us you don't have any bite marks or claw marks in the morning."

"That's a good point," Ivan chimed in. "We don't want to wake up to a toothy, hairy Kyle."

"What the hell for? Jack's an apogee. He couldn't turn me if he wanted to."

"So, they use the distance to the moon at different times to signify species?" Ivan was interested now. One of the things about Cyber Witches I've observed is their uncanny ability to find and hold knowledge. They craved it. That made Ivan a walking Google.

"I don't know about Lycans in general, I just know how Aces use those terms. Apogees are those that were turned from the bite of a perigee."

"And a perigee?" I prompted.

"They're born with the wolf inside of them. There aren't many in the world, so when they're perigee they're considered special. Shifting is easier for them and they have better control. They're not ruled by the moon when shifting, though full moons do make it hard not to shift. Bastien's a perigee, that's why his bite can turn you," he leaned forward. "Can I see the bite?"

"When we get back. I'd like it if you'd give it a good cleaning?" Another thing about Hedge Witches is their natural ability to heal.

I turned the Jeep out onto the highway and glanced at Kyle in the rearview mirror. "How did you find out Jack was a Werewolf? Was it before or after he and his G-men arrested Ivan?"

"Lycan. They like to be called Lycan because Werewolf is just too Hollywood," Kyle huffed. "It was after Jack helped us get Ivan released. We were supposed to meet up at *Le Roundup* and he didn't show. When I went looking for him at his apartment," Kyle shrugged. "I got a surprise."

"And he didn't try and eat you?" Ivan asked.

"Yeah, he did. But I'm not helpless, you *ijit.*"

Ivan laughed.

Not me. I was concerned. "Kyle, he could have hurt you, even if he couldn't turn you. Why didn't you call me?"

"You weren't exactly…" Kyle looked at the rearview mirror. "You weren't in any condition to help. It was just after you took out your dad's house."

I looked at the road. "Oh. So how did you not get eaten?"

"I had wolfsbane in the car. I'd been over to Paulette's to pick some up. Had the sample in my pocket and what do you know," he laughed nervously. "It worked."

"You're kidding," I looked back at him. "Wolfsbane protected you from him ripping you apart."

"And it worked tonight," he smiled. "Jack said it did. He could hear the others talking."

I slammed the brakes on the Jeep in the middle of the highway. Grey was abruptly deposited into the front floorboard and the two meatheads in the back hit the backs of the seats with their faces. After I threw it in park, I apologized to my mom, turned in my seat and pointed at Kyle. "You used wolfsbane out there in that Circle? In a full moon?"

Kyle looked less than happy with me. But he didn't answer.

"That means you *knew* they'd show up, didn't you?"

Ivan righted himself and turned his body to face Kyle in the small space. "Dude...is Sam right? You knew we were going to get interrupted by Werewolves?"

"Lycans," Kyle said. "And I wasn't sure. I told Jack what we were going to do and when he found out where we were going to be he warned me that was pack territory."

"That's free land. State owned."

"They don't recognize state rules or federal rules. Jack suggested I make something that'll protect us."

"He *knew* we'd need protecting."

Kyle shrugged. "He knew the pack would be out on a full moon. It made sense to me."

"But you never considered talking to me? Or Ivan? What about us? You might like getting it on with a furry man, but that might not be something Ivan and I want."

"No. Uh uh. Not into furry men," Ivan held out his hands. "Not happening. I like women. No fur."

"Why are you so mad?"

"Why shouldn't I be? Kyle...you knew there was a Werewolf—Lycan pack living right here in New Orleans. You're sleeping with one. That man suggested you use wolfsbane in a ritual because he thought we might get attacked. You knew this. Ivan and I didn't." I glanced at Ivan to make sure and he nodded his head. "That's irresponsible. You let us walk into what could have been a dangerous situation."

"But it wasn't! In fact, LeBlanc asked you for a favor."

"A favor?" I jerked my shirt and jacket away from my shoulder to expose the bloody bite and conjured a small red ball of light with my other hand so he could see. Of course the red light didn't help the appearance of the bloody shoulder. "Does this look like a favor? That bastard bit me and threatened to make me a brood mare if we can't find their people. Aren't you the least bit apologetic?"

Kyle did look a little green at the sight of my shoulder.

Sam, that symbol is glowing. You need to calm down. Breathe.

I dismissed the ball of light and put my hand to my chest and felt the warmth coming through my shirt. Mom was right. It'd been doing that every time I had a heavy emotional response to something. But neither of us had any idea *what* it meant. Was it a warning of bigger things to come if I lost my cool? Given the absence of my dad's house, I'd call that a yeah. "You tell Jack to come to the shop. I have a lot of questions for him, about *everything.*"

Kyle didn't say anything else. I took several deep breaths, with my mom coaxing me, and I started back down the highway toward home.

What I didn't know was that the pack's troubles and mine were about to become one.

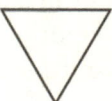

FOUR

I was expecting Jack Roberts to show up at my door later. Preferably without a fur coat and fully clothed. Unfortunately, no one told me the NOPD would be waiting on us when we arrived.

Blue and red lights illuminated the street in front of *Bell, Book and Candle* as we approached Bourbon Street. I pulled the Jeep around back and parked in the alley. We piled out of the car and hurried inside before the cops caught on that we'd slipped in without them noticing, which I didn't think was the truth because they knew all these shops had back doors.

"What do you think's going on?" Kyle asked as we made our way to the front where the main retail shop was.

"I have no freak'n idea. I just hope they don't come in here. Ivan?"

He stopped by the computer, which flipped out of sleep mode without anyone touching it. The web browser opened as page after page was displayed and then replaced by another. The cascade finally stopped on a small article in the Picayune Times Online. We piled around the computer just as the police banged on the front door. "This is the New Orleans Police Department. Open up!"

"Do I let them in?" Kyle asked.

I was scanning the article. "It's about the mutilated body in the morgue."

"Miss Hawthorne!" came Captain Prescott's voice through the door. "I can see you in there. Open this door immediately."

Ivan touched my arm. "Go. I'll keep looking."

Grey moved out of my way and kept just behind the counter as I walked fast to the door. The wards the three of us set up were in place and nothing vibrated inside of them to warn me there was any Other World threat outside the door. No crazy-ass Changelings or ninja Ghouls. I unlocked the door and opened it. Three uniformed officers flanked Captain Mildred Prescott, who stood in the center. She wore a black calf-length coat and a gray infinity scarf. Her dark eyes narrowed from the illumination coming out of the shop as Kyle turned on the interior lighting at just the right moment. "Captain Prescott, to what do I owe the pleasure of the NOPD at one o'clock in the morning?"

Unconsciously, I was looking for Crwys or Levi, some familiar face in the crowd I could latch onto and demand an explanation with my eyes. But they weren't there. I didn't know any of these uniformed officers.

Prescott held up a folded piece of paper. "We're here to collect your wolf."

Someone pulled a needle across a vinyl record. I hadn't been expecting to hear that. I didn't reach for the paper but instead leaned toward her. "What?"

"You heard me. We're here to collect your wolf." She pushed the paper into my chest, exerting enough force to move me out of her way as she preceded the uniformed men into the shop. "There it is. Just behind that counter."

I turned as another man in a dark jumpsuit stepped through. He had a rifle in his hand.

Everything happened in slow motion for the next few minutes. Ivan, Kyle and myself all moved as one to stand between the officers, the gunman, and the police captain. Luckily they all stopped, 'cause I could feel that mark in my chest burning very, *very* hot.

Mom!

Relax, baby.

"What the hell are you doing, stomping inside someone's home in the middle of the night and threatening to kill their dog?" Kyle's tone and volume was enough to put a stop to any more movement. He had a command to him when he wanted it—I'd just never seen him use it before. Seeing Jack was a good influence, maybe?

"We're not here to kill it," Prescott said with her hands on her hips.

"Well, you're not taking her without cause," Ivan said. His eyes were green and I could see him multitasking by standing in front of Grey beside me as images of documents flashed by in front of him. Now with my powers warlocked, I shouldn't be able to see that. But I could. And that was because of the Arcane. "According to this county's laws for domestic pets."

"That is not a pet," Prescott pointed at us, to where Grey stood. "That is a wolf."

I stepped forward. "That is my dog. I told you that before. She's a Husky Labrador mix. Now I suggest you tell me what the fuck is going on here before I start calling the TV stations and animal rights activists. I'm sure having them picket your precinct would boost your vote in the unpopularity department." *And if you don't get out of here, I'm not responsible for what my anger does to you or your men.*

Or us.

The officers looked at Prescott as she held up her hand. "If you'd bother to read the paper I handed you, you'd see that we're taking your wolf in for DNA testing."

I shook my head. "For what? You think she's a danger because she's big? Or you just want to be proven wrong that she's a wolf?"

"I'm surprised Holliard hasn't shared this with you. In fact, I'm surprised he's not here."

So was I. "He's not on my leash, Captain. But I am still waiting for an explanation."

"Three days ago a mutilated body was found just inside of Crescent Park. The only thing identifiable about it was the sex. Female. Two hours ago the coroner ruled the woman died from exsanguination caused by severe trauma. He identified the wounds as being caused by a wolf."

"Wolf, large dog or coyote," Ivan said.

I glanced at him and saw the ghostly image of a report in front of him.

Prescott turned her attention on him. "What?"

"The full report doesn't give specifics, does it? Dr. Taylor wrote in his report the wounds were caused by either a wolf, large dog or coyote, but it was definitely in the canine family."

Prescott took a step toward Ivan while I stared at him over her head. "And how exactly would you know the details about the coroner's report, Mr. Westerfield? Have you been hacking again?"

Luckily, Ivan caught my look and realized this wasn't the time for an *I-know-more-than-you* display. He smoothly shook his head and smiled. "No, ma'am. It was a guess on my part. The bites from any of those animals mentioned would be so similar they could be easily mistaken for one another. And Dr. Andrew Taylor is one of the best pathologists in the southeast. I can't think he'd use exacts on such an important report and have his science called into question."

I gave him an approving look as Prescott turned back to me. "Doesn't matter. I have the warrant. You're required to turn the wolf over to us."

"Not in my house I don't," I held up the paper. "It says here *Bell, Book and Candle*. This is my place of business, not my residence." *Mom, get upstairs!*

Sam...I don't think that's a good idea.

Just go. I'm not letting them take you. No one's taking you from me again.

Love and affection flooded the link between us and I had to blink a few times to stop myself from tearing up.

Another presence moved in and I could smell Bastien. <Ma petite, *are you all right? Do you need help?*> His voice was like my mom's, inside my head, but there was an echo to it, like mom's had back in the woods.

<*No. The police are here to take Grey from me.*>

<*I am coming.*>

<*No!*>

Dammit. He hung up.

Captain Prescott wasn't happy. "Fine. Then I'll arrest you."

I leaned my head back. "For what?"

"For impeding a police investigation."

"My dog did not mutilate anyone. She hasn't left my side since New Year's. Even before that. And I'll swear to it in front of a judge."

Prescott sighed. "Miss Hawthorne, either you move and let this man take the wolf, or I will do my damnedest to put that man back in jail again." She pointed at Ivan. He looked stricken.

"You getting all this, Kyle?"

Everyone looked to their right where Kyle was recording the entire event on his phone. He smiled as he moved back to get a wider shot. "Yeah I am. Especially the threats of trumped up charges."

If the threat of being filmed upset Prescott, she didn't show it. But her expression did shift from anger to something like angry concern as she approached me. I stood my ground because if she was going to attack me, I wanted it on YouTube.

"Sam..." Prescott's voice rose in something akin to panic. "What the hell happened to you?" She reached out and pulled at my jacket.

Oh no...the bite! I realized at that moment she was seeing in good lighting something I'd only glimpsed at in bad lighting. I tried to pull back from her but she grabbed my jacket at the same time, which exposed Bastien's handy work. I could only imagine what she was seeing and did an inner cringe when I realized this wasn't going to help my case and strengthen hers.

"Did that wolf do this?"

"No." I jerked away from her. I had to think of something fast. Something that would stop them from looking at my mom.

Prescott glared at me. "I order you to tell me what bit you and where you were."

"No."

The captain turned to one of the uniformed officers. "Jameson, take Miss Hawthorne into custody."

I could have hugged him when the young man in the uniform hesitated. "Ma'am?"

"You heard me. Arrest Miss Hawthorne."

"He needs to know why, Captain," I said as I tried to suppress the knot in my stomach. The night's anger, frustration, rage, irritation, surprise, fear—it was all coalescing into this mass of interconnecting bands that were being stretched to their breaking point. This insufferable woman thought she could just walk up to someone in their place of business and arrest them?

With no cause?

When Prescott didn't press the stupid order, I figured I had her on that. Her people knew their job. They were there to kidnap a wolf, not arrest the owner.

"Lloyd, get the wolf."

"No." I stepped in front of Grey. My stomach churned. I felt the heat of the mark on my chest and the bite on my shoulder. "You're *not* taking my dog."

"Samuel," Prescott pointed to the man with the rifle. "Tranquilize the damn wolf. *Now*."

My chest was on fire and the burn spread down my spine, into my arms and hands, through my legs to my feet and ignited that ball of emotion in my stomach. I thought bad things as the periphery of my vision started to burn and curl like the edges of parchment paper tossed into a flame. I zeroed in on the guy with the rifle. I wanted him to burn. I wanted him to explode into a million pieces over and over again until he was utterly destroyed.

No! Samantha, please! Don't give in!

Every fountain in the shop exploded at once. The place turned into a war zone for a few seconds as water, ceramic shrapnel and plants shot through the air. Everyone ducked down as something popped and I felt someone knock me backwards. I lay on my back as every muscle in my body locked. I couldn't move my arms, kick my legs or even turn my head. I could see Arcane glittering red all around me. It filled my lungs, cut into my flesh and burrowed into my eyes. I fought to get air into my lungs as my back arched and I realized—*I'm having a seizure!*

"Someone call an ambulance!"

"Shoot it now!"

I heard the *thufp* of the tranquilizer gun. I heard Kyle yelling something and I felt Grey on top of me. Mom was talking to me. Telling me it was going to be okay, that this was what happened when I kept building power and didn't release it. I didn't know what she was talking about as I looked into her beautiful face. She rested her head on my chest and I could move my arms and I put them around her. She was warm and I wanted to be held by her. In her arms.

Like I remembered when I was eight.

Then they were taking her from me, pulling her from me and I was screaming at them and crying, calling out for my mom. There were lights as everything moved in slow motion and a beautiful man with amber red eyes cradled my face as everything went dark.

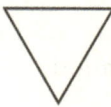

FIVE

I hated waking up in cold rooms. Under cold sheets. Especially with the sun in my eyes. When I raised my hand to block the blinding rays, I saw a needle buried deep in the top of my wrist and a clear tube taped to my skin. Crap. This usually happened at the end of a bad day, not the beginning.

I turned my head to look at the machines and then at the shadow standing in front of the window. I recognized the profile. Crwys Holliard. He had his arms crossed over his chest and his hip resting against the window's ledge. My gaze followed the lines of his body as his hips slipped into his worn out jeans. The short sleeves of the t-shirt exposed his well-toned arms.

Then there was his hair. I compared Crwys's hair to Bastien's. I don't know what it was about an edgy cut that always attracted me. Most women I knew my age liked either the short business cut or the long-haired ponytail. Not me. I liked things different. And Crwys was different. He kept his hair shaved close to his head around the back and sides, but the crown was long and hung over to one side. The cut accented his long face with its high cheekbones and squared jaw.

"You know how to strike a pose, don't you?" I sounded weird. Kinda off. Like my vocal cords had sludge on them. I coughed to clear it all out.

Crwys moved fast at the sound of my voice. He cleared the distance between us in the blink of an eye and sat on the edge of the bed as he placed a warm hand on my cheek. "Hey. You look better."

"I feel like I just ran a marathon." And then I remembered *why* I was in the hospital. I put my hands down and pushed myself into a sitting position. "They took Grey. They can't do that, Crwys. They can't take my mom like that—"

He put a finger on my lips and pursed his own as he made "sshh" noises. "Grey's okay. She's in a kennel in a local lab under quarantine. They didn't find any forensic evidence on her that connects her to the body or the bite on your shoulder."

"Of course they didn't because she didn't rip anybody apart. Stupid-ass Prescott."

Crwys pursed those sexy lips of his. "And the bite on your shoulder?"

Uhm…

"Don't stall, Sam. I can smell him all over you. Bastien LeBlanc. That bastard's marked his territory all above the ninth ward and any park he and his pack of mutts can get into. When the hell did he mark you?"

"Mark me?"

Crwys moved the hospital gown away from my shoulder. "He marked you, Sam, as his. You know he's perigee, right? He can turn you into a Lycan."

Why was it everyone else knew about this perigee and apogee and I didn't? Then again, everyone knew Werewolves were real and I had no clue. Just never ran into one before. Until now.

The look in his eyes was a bit daunting. He was close, physically close, at that moment and watching me. Waiting for an answer. So I told him. I let him know everything that happened once the wolves showed up at our ritual. Was it last night? How long had I been in the hospital?

"The bite is his way of making sure I work to find his people, and I can hear the pack."

I thought me telling Crwys would make him relax. It did just the opposite. His eyes glowed red now, the amber was gone. Everywhere he touched burned and I flinched away from him. He pulled back and then stood. His stillness unnerved me and he wasn't actually looking at me, but at something I couldn't see.

A shadow of something moved around the room and I knew I was sort of seeing him. But not quite. He was angry and this wasn't going to end well for anyone if he didn't calm down. "Crwys…please stop. Please. Don't think about what he did. Think about what I need to do. What we need to do. There's a mother and an unborn child out there depending on me. On us."

The words eventually broke through and he looked at me. Amber crept back into his eyes but he was still pissed off. I could see that in his taut muscles and thin lips. I pushed myself up and motioned for him to come back to the bed by patting the mattress. He did and he took my hand. When I flinched again from the heat he cooled down.

"Just relax. Tell me when I can pick Grey up."

He nodded. "Prescott still thinks Grey's responsible, but with no evidence to back up her suspicions, she's got to let your mom go after forty-eight hours."

"Therefore, she'll hold Grey for the full time allowed. Great." I wasn't going to feel relieved until I had Grey beside me. "So…what happened to me? How did you know I was here?"

"Levi and I arrived after a co-worker told me Prescott had taken a black and white to your shop. We got there just as you exploded. What happened is you got angry. Prescott just set you off emotionally and that triggered the Arcane. But," he held up a finger. "You reigned it in, this time. No destruction. Well, except the fountains. And yourself."

"I had a seizure."

"Yeah. You did. Prescott thought you were shot given the explosions. She's still not sure what happened with that and I'm not about to get involved in it. She's also afraid Kyle's going to release whatever it was he filmed on YouTube."

I gave him a half smile. "He should," I dropped the smile. "Are you and Levi working on the mutilated body?"

"Yeah. He and I caught it because no one else wanted it. And…"

"You sensed the body was a Werewolf?"

"Uh…" Crwys winced. "No. I didn't sense that at all. The bastard thinks she's one of his?"

"His name is Bastien."

"His name," Crwys leaned in and pressed a soft kiss to my nose. "Is bastard. And as soon as we find his people and get his pack out of our business, I'm going to kick his furry ass."

That was a fight I didn't want to see. Because honestly, I didn't know who would win. I suspected Crwys would because he'd just make Bastien go up in flames. Poof. So…I thought it was best we get off this subject and move forward. "Any idea what mutilated her? Or what it was they heard that night? You think it's Arcane in nature?"

"Dunno. There are a lot of creatures out there like the wolf. Like coyotes and dogs. But the way this kid was torn apart—" he shook his head as he thinned his lips. "I don't think it was either of those."

"Do Lycans have basic enemies?"

"Basic enemies?"

"You know, like Batman has the Penguin and the Joker, and Spiderman has Green Goblin."

Crwys laughed as he put a hand against my cheek. "Your analogies are so weird."

"That's not answering my question."

"Yes, they do. But their enemies are mostly human, and wolfsbane."

I smirked. Yeah, I already knew about wolfsbane. I just didn't know what it did…exactly. Kyle said he put it in the fire for protection. Well, it sure didn't stop Bastien from biting me.

"A Revenant or Leviathan could have done that to her because they have the strength, and when and if they want, they could have the claws."

I watched his expression. "But you don't think that's it either. In other words, you don't know what killed her."

"No," Crwys raised his shoulders. "I don't. And that's one of the reasons I stayed at the morgue. I was trying to…find out."

"By staying near her body? Crwys, you're not making sense."

"Let's just say I have a very rare talent and when I want to use it, I can speak to the dead."

Blink.

"Now don't get all freaked out. I'm not a necromancer or anything like that—"

"I hope to hell not!"

"*Sshh*, baby. Sometimes souls or spirits, whatever you want to call them, hang around. Not long. Just a few hours after the body dies at most. They get confused, not sure what just happened, but they always remember the events."

I stared at him. "And?"

"Nothing. She was gone. I need to talk to LeBlanc, and any other wolves that were there that night. I need leads other than just inferences."

I made a face. It wasn't a bad face, but it was still a face. "Are you thinking of mundane leads or magical leads?"

"*Any* leads." Crwys's phone rang and he checked the face. "Holliard," he barked into it as he put it to his cheek. He looked at me but I knew he wasn't seeing me. Then he nodded, even though the person on the other end couldn't see. "We'll be right there." He shoved his phone back into his pocket and leaned in to kiss my forehead. "They found another body."

"Mutilated?"

"Yeah. This will prove Grey's not responsible and I'll push to get her released back into your care." He grabbed a leather jacket off the back of a chair. I recognized it as a different one than the jacket he let me use. Come to think of it…where were my clothes? "I'll be back to check you out."

"Check me out? I want to go with you."

"No. You have to stay here," he kissed me again and left the room.

Screw that. I wasn't planning on staying in the hospital, bored out of my mind. The only things in hospitals were sick people, people sticking you with needles for blood and—

Morgues.

There were hospital morgues—'cause you had to have a place to cool the bodies that didn't survive—and there were stand-alone morgues like the county morgue. It would make sense if the body was in the county morgue, but it would be safer and less talked about in a hospital morgue, wouldn't it? Or was that the other way around?

Either way, it was worth a check to see if the body was here. I opened up a few of the drawers in the cabinet by the door, in the bathroom, and then opened a small closet I found behind the door. My clothes were in a bag in the bottom of the closet, along with my boots.

I undressed in the bathroom and saw the bandage wrapped around my shoulder. It went around my neck and under my arm. Chewing on my lower lip, I pulled and yanked at it, loosening the bandage enough to pull it to the side to see—

Bastien's mark.

It was there. A half sphere of dashes and then four round holes where his fangs sank in. The bite itself was clean. I leaned into the mirror get a closer look. It was scabbed over and healing, but I knew just below the surface was the Lycan venom that would start working on me pretty soon. I had maybe thirty-eight hours left.

As I changed, I noticed the mark on my chest looked less like a tattoo and more like some weird iridescent image. Almost like a club stamp that was only visible under a black light.

I didn't know if that was good, bad or indifferent.

Slipping out of the room was easy enough, the nurses were at their station busy with patients and visitors and weren't looking for fully clothed me to walk away. I raked my fingers through my long dark hair and stepped out with a purpose to the elevator. Two other people dressed in scrubs joined me inside.

"Excuse me," I began and gave them my worried face. "But do either of you know which way to the morgue?"

The smaller of the two, a middle-aged woman in teddy bear scrubs and golden skin, put her hand on my arm. "Oh no, hon. Are you here to ID a body?"

"Yes." That's it. Sound confident. Ignore that little voice in your head screaming *you're gonna get caught!*

"Morgue's always on the lower floor of the hospital," the other one said. He was tall and looked bored to death. His badge said Gerald. "Just go to the basement and the guard will take you to where you can view."

"Thank you both," I smiled at each of them and pressed the button for the basement floor. They each stepped off at earlier floors and I descended to the lowest floor alone. I was trying to come up with what story to tell this alleged guard when the elevator stopped and the doors opened.

The smell hit me first. It was a combination of disinfectant, soap and something else I couldn't identify. The elevator dumped me into a side wall facing a long hall in front of me and a right turn down another hall. I looked down both directions but didn't see a guard.

Before I could take a step down the hall to my right, a text window popped up in front of me with text bubbles.

That's the wrong way.

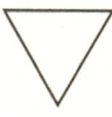

SIX

Ivan.

I looked around and up and saw a camera. "Are you spying on me?" I figured he could hear me through the hospital surveillance system.

The next text proved me right. **I was looking for the body. You showed up and I texted Kyle.**

"Is he with Jack?"

Y

"So not that way?"

No. That way is viewing and there is a guard there flirting with a nurse. Go straight ahead.

I smirked and tiptoed down the hall in front of me. There wasn't much to see, just rows of doors with names on them.

The text box moved with me. **The next one is storage.**

"Storage?" I whispered.

It's war the bodies are stored.

Then he corrected his misspelling. **Where**

I chuckled and wondered if Ivan had witchy auto correct with his Cyber Magic. "You mean like those morgue drawers?"

Sometimes. But if the drawers are full they will be stacked on gurneys in the back freezer.

Just...gross. I stopped in front of the door. Thinking ahead, I removed the jacket and wrapped it around my hand before I yanked down on the handle and opened the door. The room beyond looked like something out of a movie set. Big square with smaller squares on the back wall. There was a door on either side of me, on the adjoining walls, and then the door behind me leading back into the hall.

The jacket was becoming cumbersome so I searched the pockets and found Crwys's handkerchief. Hoping he hadn't actually wiped his nose with it, 'cause *ew*, I used it to open each of the doors. Sliding out the bodies was easy. Unzipping the bags and looking inside? That was hard. They were all hard, gray and dead.

"Well, she's not in the boxes."

Try the freezer on your left.

It was surprisingly unlocked and I stepped inside. "Can I get locked in here?"

No. It's all on an electronic system, which I've suspended for a bit. Let's hope they don't notice my tampering.

Yay for Cyber Witches. About eight gurneys were lined up side by side along the back, each with a sheet-covered body. I lifted the first three with no luck. But when I got to the fourth one, it wasn't a naked body on the gurney. It was a sealed body bag.

I hesitated at first. Did I want to see this? Did I want to have this forever burned into my brain? The answer to myself was no, but I had to solve this and get the cure before I got all hairy and toothy. I took a deep breath and slowly pulled the zipper all the way down. Then I parted the edges of the bag and looked inside.

"Lady Darksome..." I had to step back as I put my hand to my face.

Did you find her? There aren't any cameras in there.

I don't think anyone can truly explain a mutilation to anyone else. We're all set up to find different things repulsive, which makes some words, I think, subjective. I wouldn't have called this girl mutilated. I would have said she'd been butchered.

What was left of her head was little more than the outer skull at the top of what *had been* her head. There wasn't a face. Not even a jaw. And the skin and muscles had been eaten away. Her neck bone was completely exposed, as were her ribs and they were cracked and pushed inward. Her organs were gone, but I wasn't sure if that was because of what killed her or if they were removed during the autopsy.

Her legs were missing from the knees down. It looked as if they'd been ripped off. And her arms...

"Where are her arms?"

Pull her into the main room so I can see her.

"Ivan...Bastien can't see this."

I'm afraid he has to. He knows you're with the body.

"What?" I nearly shouted, but I kept my cool. Sort of. "Is he on his way here? To the morgue?"

Yep. I've been watching him through the traffic cam. The guy drives his van like he's a wolf.

Oh. Great. And some cop's going to stop him and give him a ticket on his way here. I zipped the body bag up and covered it with the sheet. The gurney had to be unlocked before I could push and pull it through the door and into the main room with the morgue drawers.

Open it back up.

"Hell no." Wait…I stopped and stared at the sheet-covered bag. I leaned in and sniffed. And then sniffed again.

That looks really weird, Sam.

"Ivan…I can *smell* Arcane. Bastien and his wolves really had smelled it."

How? With all the scents in a morgue you can pinpoint that smell?

"Yeah, I can. Do you see it?"

I didn't wait for an answer as I yanked the sheet off and unzipped the bag again. I looked with what I hoped was with my new magic…

But I didn't see anything. Not even the slightest tiny glitter of red.

I don't see anything, Sam. And…Jesus Fucking Christ…zip that back up.

I heard the revulsion in Ivan's text and then looked at the text box. It wasn't there. "Ivan…I can *hear* you."

That's not possible. I'm not projecting through the system's speakers. If I did that, everyone in the hospital could hear me.

"Well, I heard you. I can hear your voice. Yeah, you sound a bit electronic, like you're using a reverb machine, but…your text box is gone."

He didn't answer right away and I zipped the bag back up. Apparently Ivan's magic was still growing and evolving. "Ivan, are you in the system?"

If you mean am I immersed, yes.

"Just like Kennett was when he died?"

Sort of. But I know when to get out. You think that's why you can hear me without the text?

"I don't know. Could be the Arcane. So can you—"

Wait. His presence disappeared. I don't know how to explain it; I just knew he wasn't watching me anymore. He wasn't in the hospital system. Then, **LeBlanc's outside. I just told Kyle how to get him to where you are.**

Great. I cautiously moved out of the storage room and into the hall. To my left were the elevators and to my right was another door that looked like it led outside. I ran toward it and looked through the door's wired glass window in time to see a white van pull up in the parking lot.

I almost didn't recognize Bastien with his clothes on. But I sensed him, even through the shut door. He was this *presence* that wouldn't go away. He wore dark jeans, boots, a red shirt and a denim jacket. From where I stood, he looked like a farm hand. A very sexy one too. This dude really should pose for the covers of bodice ripper romance books.

I have control of the alarm and the electronic locks. Open the door for them.

I needed to put a little weight behind the door but I got it cracked in time for Bastien to wrench it the rest of the way. I stumbled outside and into his arms. Looking up into his half smiling face was sort of a reward. "Hey, Bastien."

"*Bonjour, ma petite.* Are you all right? That *diable* prevented me from seeing you when you were admitted here."

Diable? A devil? He must've meant Crwys. "I ah…yeah, I'm fine."

He brushed my hair and I backed away. Was it me or was I more attracted to him now than I had been last night?

"May we see the body?"

I motioned for him to follow me. Kyle was the last through the door and quietly closed it. Ivan might be able to silence alarms, but he couldn't exactly arrange physical silence. There was still a guard around the corner.

Jack was quick behind Bastien as they came into the storage room where I'd left the gurney. Jack looked nice too. I had only seen him in his G-man suit, and naked, but today he wore jeans and a dark blue hoodie. His Vans were the same color as the hoodie. I guess gay wolves were as fashion coordinated as their non-wolf counterparts.

Kyle was in his usual black uniform. Black pants, black shirt and black peacoat. We really needed to discuss the color wheel.

Bastien stood in front of the gurney but he didn't move to touch it. His expression was sad and I took it upon myself to unzip the bag a third time and spread it open.

His reaction wasn't the one I expected. Although, I wasn't sure

PHAEDRA WELDON

what reaction I'd expect from a wolf. Maybe crying, howling or even a tear?

This guy leaned in and sniffed.

My stomach flopped. I smelled the Arcane again.

He sniffed again and motioned Jack over. Jack also leaned in and sniffed. Then he reached in and ran his bare finger over one of the bare, exposed bones and stuck it in is mouth.

After I slapped my hand over my mouth to prevent myself from dry-heaving, I looked at Kyle. Good. He looked as green as I felt 'cause I bet he'd been kissing that mouth.

"She is not wolf."

What? I imagined the sound of a needle being dragged across a vinyl record again. I leaned to the side and looked up at Bastien. "What do you mean she's not wolf?"

"*Chérie*, this is not a Lycan," he wrinkled his nose as he sniffed it again. "It smells like human…like wolf but…"

"It's too human," Jack filled in from his side of the gurney. He moved to the left and sniffed again. "Whatever this is, it isn't right."

I had two Lycans sniffing a ravaged corpse, telling me the body wasn't right. I absently rubbed at my chest before I gestured to the gurney in a circular manner. "So you're both telling me this girl isn't a Lycan?"

"She's…" Bastien screwed his handsome face up into something akin to a worried expression. "She's not, *not* Lycan. But she's not all Lycan." He finally shook his head and looked at Jack. *"Pischouette, mal pris?"*

Jack shook his head and shrugged. "I'll say."

I pointed to Bastien. "I didn't catch that last bit." I was pretty good with Acadian most of the time, but there were words when pronounced that just slipped right by.

He gestured to the body. "The little girl was caught in mid shift. She…she's stuck, not making it either way."

I think he means the girl was stuck between being human and being Lycan.

Staring at the mutilated mess, I sighed. "So, she was an apogee?"

Jack nodded. Bastien shook his head.

A turned wolf, but not turned enough. "Can you tell who might have done this to her?"

"Normally—yeah," Bastien scratched the back of his head. "But this…I don't recognize this."

"When I was turned," Jack said, taking up the slack. "Bastien knew who turned me without me ever saying. In fact he knew before I did and sought me out. But this…" He shook his head at the body.

"Smells bad," Bastien made a face and zipped the body bag up.

I wondered, "Bastien, what do you smell that's bad? Can you describe it?"

"Yeah, like rotten chicken. Like when I don't take out the garbage," he pointed at me. "It's like your magic, but it's not."

Bingo! Arcane. I'd discovered over the years that smells could on occasion be subjective, but not with Arcane. Everyone described it the same way. I smelled it because I'm a Witch. *Was* a Witch?

Still a Witch…technically. And I figured Bastien and Jack smelled it because of their keen canine noses.

Sam—the guard is heading your way. You got a second to get that body back where it goes and hide.

Kyle and I relayed Ivan's message. It took us less than that second to get the gurney back in the freezer and us hidden in the back. We waited until Ivan gave us the all clear. Once we had that, I walked them out the back door to the van.

"Want a lift back to the shop?" Jack asked. "I don't think Bastien would mind seeing where you worked."

"Yeah…" I hesitated getting in the back as I looked at the door we'd just stepped out of.

"Sam, what is it?" Kyle asked.

"Crwys got a call while we were in the hospital. They found another body. Which means there's another player out there that not only might have kidnapped Bastien's people, but they're using Arcane to shift humans into beasts."

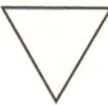

SEVEN

"Two bodies?" Kyle said as Bastien pulled the van around the back of *Bell, Book And Candle* and shut off the engine. "Where's the other body?"

I stepped out of the back along with Kyle, followed by Jack and Bastien. The January afternoon was cool enough to put a chill in the air and I noticed it had rained while I was in the hospital. It was two o'clock the following day, Thursday, and the sky threatened more rain, along with the aberrant ray of sunshine bursting through over the city. I smelled fish and oil as I shuffled up to the back of the shop and unlocked the door and keyed the alarm.

I absently reached down to stroke Grey's neck—and freaked out a little when she wasn't there. Now my brain was not only flooded with erroneous questions about what kind of creature was in the morgue, but seriously bad thoughts on how to make Mildred Prescott's life a living hell if I didn't get Grey back soon.

This was just not me. I didn't really consider revenge a great strategy in any situation. Yeah, I'm like anyone else when it comes to the reaction of someone doing me wrong. I want to get even the same as the next person. But usually that anger melts and I'm on to the best way to remedy the situation. Part of me knew this new body Crwys was investigating would prove Grey's innocence, and I trusted my detective to bring her home to me.

But this other part of me, the one lurking in the darkest closet of my mind, the one that crept along the shadows of my imagination and utterly destroyed the bodies of my dad, my step-mom and their nurse, as well as their house, that part of me was already thinking of curses, finding a disreputable Vodoun Priestess in the Quarter, or summoning a Fetch and sending it out to punish her myself.

These thoughts just weren't me! But there they were, jumping up into my window frame like a pen full of popcorn kittens. Each one leaping up to snag my attention for a brief moment before I shoved it back down.

Were those thoughts the Arcane that now permeated my insides? Were they caused by the symbol on my chest? Was I ever going to find the answers without getting myself and everyone I know in trouble?

Or worse.

Kyle went through the shop and turned on the lights before heading through the door into the retail area. I stopped at the break room and rinsed out the kettle before I filled it and set it back on its warmer. I pressed the button and turned to Jack and Bastien as Kyle came back through.

"I turned the lights on but left the closed sign out," he stood by Jack and crossed his arms. "What other body?"

I looked at each of them, more aware of Bastien's golden gaze than the others. He had a power about him. It was there, like a subtle hum just below the skin. He also exuded an odd calm. Calm men weren't something I was used to, especially since Crwys always felt like he was on the verge of fighting.

"All he said was they caught another mutilated body, and he was sure this would prove Grey had nothing to do with the first one," I looked at the floor. "I just want her home."

"This will happen, *chérie*," Bastien said. Even his voice had a hint of calm to it. This amazed me, given I'd seen him covered in fur and teeth less than twenty-four hours ago. "She will be home soon. Or I will personally rip the throat out of anyone who cages her."

I smiled at Bastien and put my hand on his arm. "There will be no ripping of throats, okay? There's been enough ripping of a lot of things. Especially flesh, given what we all just saw in that morgue." I had to put on my serious face, and my serious attitude now. I also needed to talk to Crwys and get information on what he found at that call. Given our previous conversation, I was sure he'd call me once he found out I wasn't in the hospital anymore and I'd skipped out on the bill. Oops.

What I didn't want was him coming by while the wolves were in the shop. Though he said he wanted to talk to the wolves, I wasn't so sure the puppies should meet *Mister Flame On*.

Jack walked from around the table and pulled down four mugs.

He also pulled out the tea sampler Kyle picked up a week ago and set it on the table. "I think we need to take a moment to think about the implications. Have some tea and put our heads together?"

Bastien snorted before he pointed at Jack. "Apogee."

"You say that like it's a dirty word," I said.

"Not a dirty word. Just is. Jack's turning was the mistake of Marilla's *frére*."

I wanted to make sure I understood what Bastien just said as Jack took the now heated kettle off its stand and poured equal amounts of hot water in each mug. "Marilla is the missing female?"

"*Oui*."

"And her brother is responsible for turning Jack?"

Bastien nodded. Suddenly he looked tired, almost like a parent at their wit's end as he rubbed at his face. "*Oui*. Lucas is perigee, same as his *soeur*. Only perigee can make a *chiot*."

"*Chiot?*"

"Me," Jack said as he set the kettle back on its stand. "Apogees who accept the pack and the pack accepts them are known as *chiot*, or pups, because we're turned. Those that are young and born are called *loup de chiot*. There is a preference given to the perigee, but from what I've been able to learn, perigee aren't born as often as they once were. For every twenty children born to the perigee, maybe one *is* perigee and the others are human. In this area, the Lycans' numbers have been declining fast for the past fifty years, so they've been forced to selectively choose those to carry on and create apogee."

"Can apogee have perigee?" The words felt odd on my tongue.

Bastien answered with a nod. "But the births, they are as rare as any perigee couple. Arduinna has much in store for us, but we don't know why she wants so few of us."

There was that name again. I needed to educate myself where Arduinna fit into the pantheon of myths I'd grown up with. The world was filled with so many of them, from the Greeks to the Norse, the Native American to even the Witches. Similarities in names as well as positions and attributes bled from culture to culture and I accepted the old adage that all the Gods and Goddesses were one.

But I was having a bit of trouble accepting that a Goddess whose patronage was wolf-people had a shared pantheon with my own. I didn't think it was because I was stingy with my own Gods and Goddesses, it was just…Witches and wolves? How urban fantasy-esque was that?

The back door opened before I asked my question about Arduinna.

Sam!

My heart melted into my insides, making my middle gooey and golden as Grey came running from the back. I knelt down and scooped her into my arms as she nipped, licked and whined aloud, all the while talking to me. *Oh I missed you! They fed me dog food. Dog food! As if I were some ordinary canine in such a foul place. And speaking of foul places—wait until I tell you where they stuck things!*

Bastien's rich, deep laughter made a nice accompaniment to Mom's non-stop complaining. I realized she was broadcasting to the entire pack.

Then that laughter twisted and became a howl. A dark, spine chilling howl. Grey and I pulled back from our place on the floor as Bastien turned. I stood up as he moved in front of me in a protective stance.

Jack took an almost comical growling stance by the counter as the two faced the back.

Crwys and Levi stepped into view; both of them wearing some seriously bored expressions at the display. Crwys was the first to approach. His eyes were red; Levi's were hidden behind shades.

"Easy there, puppies." Crwys said as he moved around the table and approached me from behind. He was quick and slipped his arm around my waist. "We're not the enemy here. But you and me," he said as he pointed at Bastien with his free hand. "We are going to have a lesson on marking another man's woman."

Wait...what?

Jack was the one that spoke. "*Diable du feu*," he said in a thick voice. He looked like he was mentally caught in between, as if he wanted to shift but wouldn't or couldn't. It reminded me of the condition of the girl's body in the morgue.

Levi laughed as he joined us at the table. He put his hands on the back of one of the chairs, standing just a few feet from Jack. Levi is a beautiful man. Physically, he reminded me a lot of the actor Michael Ealy. He wore nice suits, liked to follow the rules and always wore shades. I didn't know if the shades were an affectation due to his allergy to sunlight, or because he looked good in them.

"Told you, 'Lo," Levi said as he removed his shades and revealed his incredible blue eyes. "I'm not *diable* to a Lycan. That's you."

Levi had started calling Crwys 'Lo a lot lately and I couldn't figure out why. When I asked Crwys, all he would say was it was a childhood name.

"You shouldn't be here," Bastien pointed at Crwys.

"Neither should you, Lassie. The agreement was you stay in your woods and it stays government protected land."

Lassie? I stepped back from Crwys and looked at him like he'd lost his freak'n mind. Yeah, Crwys was tall and wiry and sexy, but Bastien was a good foot and a half taller, and he's a wolf.

Let me repeat—he is a *wolf!*

Bastien looked from Crwys to me and back to Crwys. "*Ma petite* was yours?"

Crwys pulled me close to him. "Is."

Bastien stepped forward and let loose a growl before he said, "I offer a challenge. For the right of *petite.*"

Crwys stood up straight and sneered. "I accept."

I pushed back and held out my hands. "Whoa, both of you. Wait a second. No one consulted me on this. I date whom I choose, not the other way around. And before we start showing who's got the bigger balls, we have a job to do because whether you like it or not, Mr. LeBlanc, I do not want to be your mate. Got it?" I glared at Bastien. "Got it?"

"*Oui.*"

Crwys snorted.

I whirled on him. "And *you*…be nice. Don't think this is over. I plan on finding out why Jack called you a fire demon."

He grinned and I was happy to see the amber return to his eyes. "Jack is mistaken. And you can't possibly think I'm going to trust this schmuck after he forcibly marked you."

"She didn't fight."

I pointed at Bastien. "Stop it! I didn't know what you were doing." I grabbed an English breakfast tea and started steeping it. Bastien grabbed a honey lemon and Jack grabbed a chai. All of this was done in silence, except for Mom talking to me about her ordeal and the four of them giving each other ugly looks. No one said another word out loud until we were seated at the table, each with a mug of tea. I made sure I sat away from both of the big boys.

"The body in the morgue isn't one of the Aces. She isn't even a full wolf." I sipped my tea and let the warmth do its job.

Bastien finished his tea and stood to refill the kettle and start it heating again.

Levi held up his hands. "You guys were in the morgue?"

Everyone nodded. I said, "Yeah, I was looking for the body when Ivan—"

Wait…where was Ivan?

Speaking his name brought him to the forefront of everyone's mind. Grey was on the floor beside my chair and perked her head up as well.

"Sam," Kyle said. "Have you talked to him since the morgue?"

"Ivan was in the morgue too?" Crwys asked. The two cops did not look happy.

"He was in the security system," I said to Crwys before I turned to Kyle. "No. I haven't."

"I'll call," Kyle retrieved his phone.

"Back up," Crwys said. "Ivan broke into the hospital security system so you could go looking for the mutilated body."

I frowned at him. "You're learning our M.O."

"Do you know how many laws he broke doing that?"

I stared at Crwys. Since when was this guy worried about rules? "Ivan's good at what he does. Are you afraid they'll catch him?"

"Aren't you?"

A shrug was my best answer. "No. I trust him. Look, why are you so weirded out?"

Crwys stood and came around the table to offer me his hand. "We need to talk in private. Please?" he asked.

I took it and stood. He led me toward my office, away from the break room area. I felt Bastien's eyes on us and glanced over at him. He looked…irritated. Crwys turned us around so that my back was to Bastien. "Sam, think about this. It occurs to me, or maybe I'm just suspicious by nature, that the Magical Parliament is more interested in keeping your Elemental Gifts locked up. They passed them around the table like party favors. That gives them the false sense of security that you're power*less*," his gaze searched my face. "They have the copy of the Hammer. They dismissed the charges against Arden, and have made a public statement that you were incorrectly accused. But you're *still* warlocked. Aren't you the least bit curious why?"

"I figured they were just slow to admit they were in the wrong."

"Babe, you've got something inside that's slowly taking hold of you, making you far more dangerous than you were before the warlocking."

My eyes narrowed. "What are you saying?"

"I'm saying that your Elemental power is what kept the Arcane in check. But now that your natural power's been stripped," Crwys's voice had lowered considerably. "Arcane is free to do what it wants. And the sad part about this is if the Parliament knew you had this thing inside of you, they never would have warlocked you. They'd have just killed you. My suspicion is that someone suspects you do have Arcane and they're stopping your Elementals from controlling it, hoping you'll somehow betray your use of something they view as highly forbidden. I don't know who, but you can bet you're being watched. I think it's a good idea not to be so visible until the warlocking is removed."

"My Elementals were the ones keeping the Arcane in check?" I put my hand on his hand. "How do you know this? How would anyone in Parliament know this? What are you not telling me? And don't say you're not keeping something from me because you really don't lie very well."

The amber in his eyes vanished and they became a soft, pinkish red. "Witches have successfully hidden their use of Arcane for centuries, Sam. As long as their God Mother's Gifts remain intact. It's the ones that lose those Gifts that go crazy, the ones history remembers. The ones the Parliament and all manner of creature in all the worlds want to destroy. I'm saying if you don't get those damn little creatures back, Parliament isn't the only thing out there that's going to want you. Alive or dead."

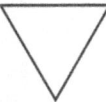

EIGHT

I knew on some level he was right about the Arcane because I could feel it. It had a voice now that it didn't have before. A small, niggling ghost in the back of my mind. It came to me when I made that house and the bodies vanish. It came to me when I destroyed what had been left of Ronald Kennett. I could hear it now, telling me Crwys was wrong, that the Elementals had no power over me or over anything I wanted to do.

I blinked several times to clear my head, to banish that voice and concentrate on what Crwys was trying to tell me. "Other than Parliament?"

"Sam...Arcane is feared and sought after. Yes, Levi's demon comes from the same realm, and he has the same power but being bonded with Levi's soul is what keeps that power in check. Leviathans—"

"Leviathans don't have the bond," I finished for him. "They use their power in this world."

"And they're attracted *to* it. Don't think that Dionysus isn't aware of what's happening to you. He pulled your strings to get you to the place to actually use it, Sam. That's what started this. So for now, you've got to do everything in your power to play nice and get those Elementals back," he put a hand to my face. "Don't blind yourself to the possibility that his ultimate goal was to infuse you with Arcane, and then take your body. Think of the power he would have then and your soul to ride."

We heard a low growl and I immediately looked behind me. Bastien's eyes burned gold and he snarled just loud enough to hear. When I turned back to Crwys, he had his middle finger up, saluting the Alpha. Dammit. I did not want a fight in my shop. The difference in their body weight and height was significant. Strength wise, I was pretty sure Bastien could stomp Crwys into the ground. Agility wise— I'd seen Crwys move at lightning speed and was pretty sure he could out maneuver the Lycan. But when it boiled right down to it, we didn't have time for this testosterone shit.

And my shop didn't either. I'd just got it fully restocked and making money again after last month's disaster. I wasn't counting the fountain inventory I'd destroyed yesterday. I assumed Kyle had taken care of it.

I grabbed Crwys's hand and pulled it down. "All right. Stop it. You're both pretty." I moved away from Crwys and back to the table. I'd heard what he said, about Dionysus watching me, plotting through time to fashion the ultimate body to steal, and I didn't want to think about that at this minute. I was doing a total Scarlet O'Hara and putting if off till tomorrow. "Right now we need to address the fact that Ivan—"

The door to the back came open and in walked Ivan with two bags and a wide grin. "Hey! Sorry I'm late. I had to pick up food. I was starving so I brought Chinese for everyone—oh hi Crwys, Levi." He glanced at me with surprise before he put the bags on the table.

It was the good stuff from Moon Wok. Jack and Kyle expressed their joy and started grabbing paper plates and silverware, as well as chopsticks from the kitchen shelves. My own stomach growled when Ivan handed me a carton of house lo mein, complete with chopsticks and a fork.

"I am sorry I'm late getting back. But when I dive like that into the Cyber World, I am seriously famished afterward." He pointed to the second bag he'd moved to the side of the table. "That's *my* food."

I'd seen Ivan hungry. Given the time and opportunity he would eat the entire bag, regardless of how much food was in it.

I shook my head as he winked and approached his bag. I also spotted Bastien sniffing the air. He moved around Jack and Kyle as they spooned out portions of what looked like sweet and sour chicken and garlic chicken, then stood next to Ivan, sniffing him. I thought for a minute he was going after whatever was in Ivan's bag. Ivan turned when he realized the big guy was sniffing him and stepped away.

"What the hell?"

Bastien stopped and gave Ivan the biggest shit-eating grin I'd ever seen. He clapped Ivan on the back and said, "*Très bien, mon ami.*"

Kyle held up his hand. "English guys. What's wrong with Ivan?"

Crwys stood beside me and put his arms around my middle, with me still holding the box of noodles. "He said very good, my friend."

I pushed his arms away before I poked at my noodles with my chopsticks. "We just don't know what is very good. The food?"

"That's not important," Ivan declared and was looking a little red. "Let's just get to whatever you guys were talking about before I got here."

Crwys snorted. "He had sex," he pointed to Bastien. "And the *tayeau* there can smell it."

I knew the word. It meant hound. I'd never considered it offensive before, until I saw Bastien jump over the table in a flash and attempt to put his hands around Crwys's neck. Notice I said attempt. I dropped my noodles getting out of the way (dammit) and Bastien slammed into the fridge because Crwys wasn't there anymore. Bastien turned and searched the room. "*Diable!*"

Crwys came down the stairs from my apartment and stopped on the last one. "I have been called worse. Now I would suggest, *tayeau petite*, you knock it off. Do you really want Sam to find your missing people?"

Bastien snarled at Crwys. "If she doesn't, she's *mine*."

"Stop it. Now!" That last burst had a bit of power behind it. The room filled with red glitter—a tiny amount really—which faded immediately, but it made everyone stop. "No more name calling, and no more goading. Let's just get this shit done." I retrieved my noodles and my chopstick and started eating. Thirty second rule. Sue me. After a few bites of euphoria at the incredible taste of the lo mein, not to mention the satisfaction in my stomach because I couldn't remember the last time I ate, I waved to get everyone's attention. "I think the next step should be having Bastien and Jack, or one or the other, take a look at the body you found today." I looked at Crwys.

He immediately shook his head. "There's no way I can get these two in there to view a body."

"Crwys, these two sniffed the first body. Let them sniff the second and we can be sure if this is a serial mutilation."

"You can't argue with that, *diable*," Bastien said as he grabbed a box of house fried rice and a fork. I was amazed at how carefully he ate. He was almost dainty the way he held his fork and made a point of not spilling a single grain of rice.

Kyle spoke up. "They could put out a missing persons report.

What could it hurt? Get their faces on the street and make sure to mention she's pregnant."

"No publicity," Bastien and Crwys said in perfect unison. They looked at each other, scowled and then looked away.

I set my box on the counter. "Crwys, just arrange a viewing. Call in a favor or something. You want to find the one responsible, don't you?"

He looked at me for a while as the amber returned to his eyes. "I'll see what I can do," he looked at everyone else. "But I can't take all of you."

"I'll stay here," Ivan said as he ate. "I got some things to do." When everyone looked at him, he frowned. "What? The shop hasn't been open all day and I spent several hours last night cleaning up the fountain mess," he smirked at Kyle. "Someone was too emotionally distressed to help me."

That I could believe.

"This was before you spent time with the lady?" Bastien said.

Ivan blushed bright red as Crwys, Kyle, Jack and Levi started in on their guy-ribbing.

So that was why Bastien sniffed Ivan. I couldn't help but grin at the boy. So Ivan had sex. I made an assumption he accessed the morgue's security system from this girl's home. That was a much better excuse than hunger—though from the way he was scarfing down his Chinese, hunger was a definite factor. The truth to be found was whether it was the sex that made him hungry or the cyber diving.

Or both?

"We will be there to represent the pack," Bastien said through a mouthful of food and getting us back on topic.

"Why can't just one of you go?" Crwys's tone wasn't as antagonistic as it had been.

"I am the Alpha," Bastien put his hand on his chest. "I lead. Jack is learning from me."

I nodded. "Makes sense. I'm going. Kyle?"

"I'd like to go where Jack goes."

Aww. I just felt all mushy inside. No really. I'm serious. I was shocked this romance had lasted past four hours. And even though I was still a little worried that Jack would wolf-out and really hurt Kyle, at least he wouldn't turn him. I wasn't sure how Kyle's aunt Arden would take to having her nephew turned into an apogee Lycan.

My ears felt like they needed to pop and I did the customary swallow to pop them. That didn't work. Bastien put his food down and backed away just as Jack jumped up and his chair fell back. Both of them were holding their ears. I looked at Kyle who'd gone very, very white. He looked back at me with both his hands on the table. "Someone's put a cap on the area."

Oh Sweet Lady! That could only mean the Clerics were coming. Like an ill wind or smell those fuckers liked to disarm every magical entity and spell within an area before they arrived. I'd have known that if I had my Elemental Gifts because they would have been inaccessible to me. Though my Sylph had managed to slip by their cap last time the four of them came together.

A presence pressed against my skin. It moved around me and settled in the base of my skull like a tension headache.

Crwys started putting the food back in a bag and gesturing for everyone to get up. "We need to get Google boy and the dogs out of here."

"Why?" Bastien demanded.

"Because if they're here about Sam's warlocking, we need to not be a distraction. I'm leaving too," he handed the bag to Kyle. "I'll give you a call when I have a viewing time and you can coordinate a meeting with everyone."

Kyle took the bag but shook his head. "I'm not leaving Sam. Not after what they did to her."

Crwys shrugged. "Just don't mess this up for her, okay? Just in case Parliament made a decision," he turned to Bastien. "You really need to go."

The big man looked at me and I smiled with a pleading look. "I will go, but Jack will stay. He is an apogee, and not easily detected. He will protect Samantha."

Jack nodded to Bastien. "I will give my life for the Alpha's mate."

"I am not his mate!" I yelled out.

Ivan was already packed up and out the door in front of Crwys and Bastien. All that remained was Kyle, Jack and I.

"Ever met a Cleric Hive, Jack?"

He shook his head as he pushed his chair back under the table and straightened his shirt. "Not officially. But I know about them because of what Kyle's told me."

"Brace yourself," I said as I headed for the door to the retail shop. Grey crowded in beside me, not letting me out of her sight. "'Cause they can be real pissers."

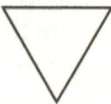

NINE

The Hive stood in the center of my shop when we walked in from the back, just like I knew they would be. It didn't take magic to know some people used the same old tricks because they worked. Showing their victim there was no way to keep them out was their oldest intimidation trick. What I hadn't counted on was seeing Cromwell Dryden, the Grand High Master, with them, making them a force of five instead of four. Elemental Magic worked around the basics of life—Earth, Air, Fire and Water. When combined, these Elements came together to make Spirit, which I had a rudimentary control over before the warlocking.

They all wore their cloaks closed with the hoods up, their representative or sponsored Elements visible as pendants on chains around their necks. All except Cromwell, who led them toward me without his hood up and his robe open. I knew the names of two of the others. Their sponsored Fire was named Fred. Nasty-ass who hated me because my mom, the southeast's best Tracker, was responsible for putting Fred's father in a warlock.

Their Earth sponsor was Emily Pearson. We'd met in an unofficial capacity at a fundraiser held at Arden Vervain's house. The other two I simply called Mister Air and Miss Water. I think I heard Mister Air's name once before, but I couldn't for the life of me remember it at that moment. Miss Water's cloak wasn't as well buttoned as the others and I could see her pointy cheek below the hood's shadow.

Grey sat at my feet when I stopped just past the counter. Kyle and Jack moved in to the right and stood behind the counter beside Ivan's computer.

"This isn't a meeting for Cowens," Cromwell said. His voice was

52

deep, steady, and didn't really telegraph any sort of emotion. Not even irritation.

I put my hands on my hips. "You didn't call first. He's my company. I hope you're here to remove the warlock?"

I could see on Cromwell's face that wasn't why they were here. And that just set my tone for the rest of this impromptu meeting. "Well...I see. I'm to remain locked out when I never committed a crime."

"If you didn't commit a crime, then where's your dad?" That was Fred. He still had his hood up but I knew his voice. He stood to Cromwell's left, probably there so the Grand High Master could keep an eye on him.

"Keep your tongue," Cromwell said.

"But look at her sir," Fred kept on going. "She's been warlocked for a month and she looks fine. My dad's health failed in less than two weeks. But she's up walking, talking and running around the city. She's even been meeting with Lycans."

Well, that bit of knowledge coming out of Fred's mouth surprised me. The only way he'd know that was if he'd been spying on me. I made a mental note to sic Ivan on this bastard's ass.

-Why have Ivan do what you can do better?-

I froze for a second at that voice and looked down at Grey, but she was looking at the Clerics. *Mom, did you just say something?*

Now she did look up at me. *No. What's wrong?*

"Samantha," Cromwell said at that moment and brought my attention back to him. "It has been brought to our attention, and I do mean the higher ranking members of Parliament, that you haven't suffered from the warlock. Not physically, not astrally, not even mentally."

A tiny fire of anger ignited in the pit of my stomach. "As I said, you warlocked an innocent Witch, with no proof of any wrong doing, and now you're disappointed because I'm not suffering? What the hell is wrong with you people? What is your point, Cromwell? I didn't do anything wrong. I heard you have your damn book. You didn't find it on me, near me or around me. In fact, I don't know *where* you found it. But you warlocked me on suspicion of stealing it." I held out my arms. "Where is my justice for being wrongly accused?"

"You can't talk to the Grand High Master like that!" Fred threw back his hood and took several very angry steps forward.

He was immediately stopped by a wave of Cromwell's hand.

Fred went flying backwards and I thought for a second he would go through my store's front window. But he didn't. He just hung there, suspended above the floor.

"This is officially your second warning, Fred. If you do anything like that again, raise a hand to Miss Hawthorne or even make noise as if you were going to, you will be warlocked with no possibility of return." He pivoted and looked at his hanging prisoner. "Do I make myself clear?"

Fred nodded vigorously. But Cromwell didn't let him loose. He just hung there the whole time.

"I am sorry, Samantha, for Fred's outburst."

"I know. He hates me because of my mother."

Really? Who is that kid?

I sent back a quick explanation. *He says you had his father warlocked and it killed him.*

I've had many bad seeds warlocked, Sam-Sam. His name is Fred? No last name?

Not that I can remember. I refocused on Cromwell. "I'm waiting for an answer."

"The answer is why we're here. It has come to our attention that a very special Codex has disappeared. It was part of a collection of Arcane artifacts held by one of the Elders who...passed away last month. The Codex itself, like the Malleus Maleficarum, is unreadable. But its purpose, as we've come to learn, is to infuse all of the God Mother's children with Arcane."

I blinked at him because that wasn't what I expected him to say. I noticed how he down played the Elder deaths, which I knew were committed by Kennett, as *passing away*. Truth was, the fools were made into Shadow People by Kennett and used to terrorize a group of human children stolen by my aunt. Well, the Leviathan riding her body.

Ignoring Fred the Hangman, I looked at each one of them for a few seconds before resting my gaze on Cromwell again. "And?"

Cromwell gave me a tight smile. "It was suggested by Parliament that you could pay back some of the service they believe you owe by finding this Codex and returning it to them. After all, your mother was an excellent Tracker. Perhaps the ability is inherent within you as well."

I opened my mouth to say something, then closed it, then opened it again. I really had to put this into perspective. "So...I've been wrongly warlocked. You admit that. But instead of just removing it, you want me to find a Codex to somehow make up time I owe in service."

Cromwell gave me a half smile.

"How am I supposed to find something without my Elementals?"

Emily spoke up. She had my Gnome. "You're very apt at finding your way around difficult situations. As you were told before, Parliament wants a year of service from you. I would like to test your abilities."

"Bullshit."

-They suspect something.-

This time I looked around the room, which was a bad thing to do in front of five Clerics.

"Sam?" Kyle said to my right.

"Sorry. There's a gnat in here. I hate gnats." Bad lie. But I had to think fast because there was no way I was telling these people I was hearing voices.

Emily said, "It's not bullshit, Samantha. Cromwell is the Grand High Master of Parliament. If he wants proof before he removes the warlock, then he can ask for proof."

"You people want me to provide the proof while I'm warlocked. *That's* the bullshit part, Emily." I narrowed my eyes at her. "Putting me out there to find this Codex, if it is what you say it is, with no magic, is like giving someone a raw steak to chum the water and telling them to capture the shark. With their bare hands. Give me back my Elementals and I'll be better equipped to defend myself."

When they looked at each other and didn't say anything, I got a little worried. Glancing at Jack and Kyle, I said, "What? Did something happen to my Elementals?"

"Oh, no," Cromwell said a bit too forcefully. "I want you to prove to me you're capable of a simple retrieval."

"You mean you want me dead. Because that's what'll happen." I didn't think finding some Codex was going to be that hard. Kyle had spells to look for magical items, and if it was an Arcane item, Ivan would be able to see it, and so would I.

I just couldn't shake the feeling there was something they weren't telling me. But I knew I wasn't going to get much more out of them.

Fred twitched. I hope he fell, and I was very happy he didn't have my Salamander.

"I have conditions."

Cromwell raised his hand. "I will remove the warlock when you succeed."

"That's not all, and don't think I won't hold you to that. I'm already considering my own counsel, and you know any magical lawyer in the country would request a Tribunal."

All five of them reacted to that. If there was one thing any Cleric hated, it was the group of Witches hired to watch the Clerics. Clerics were held to a higher standard than everyone else. And the Tribunal Members?

Practically saints. With no patience.

A Tribunal assumes the bringer is innocent and the punishers must prove their actions were justified.

"There's no need to take things that far." Cromwell looked irritated.

"Yes there is, because you people haven't made any sense from the moment you came to warlock me. As for my other condition," I pointed to the ground. "This is it. No more. No more service and no more poking your noses into my business. And no more just busting in here without my permission."

"I can only assure removal of the warlocking."

"Then you better get the rest of my requests approved. Because I'm not looking until I have all of it in writing. With everyone's signatures."

"That's ridiculous!" Mister Air shouted. Yay. Because he knew, like they all knew, if I had it in writing, I could bind them to it.

Cromwell looked as if he were about to answer when Emily spoke up. "Where is your father? Where is his house? Or his wife? Or the nurse that took care of your father?"

I wasn't prepared to answer that so I just stared at her.

-Tell them they are in a better place.-

I almost answered that voice out loud and told it to shut up.

"Why are you hesitating, Sam?"

"Because I don't know."

"But you're aware the house he lived in is missing."

I didn't say anything. Grey leaned in close to me.

Cromwell spoke up. "The lot where the house stood is empty, Samantha. The house hasn't been bulldozed or torn down. It was never built. It's as if it never existed. The neighbors we talked with don't recall there being a house on that corner. It's been an empty lot since the subdivision was built."

I tried to keep what I was feeling inside from showing on the outside. What I remembered most about my dad was that he always knew when I was lying…because I was bad at it. My expression always told on me. And I sure as hell didn't want it telling on me now.

"You don't look upset or surprised."

"I haven't been there in a long time. I don't know what it looks like. You sure you have the address right?"

Cromwell took a step toward me and put a finger under my chin. He lifted my head so I would look up at him. "I suspect you know more than you're willing to tell. But if this matter were brought up before the Parliament, I am more than sure that without answers, that warlock would never be removed. So let us just agree that you will find the Codex and I will remove the warlock."

I pulled back and glared at him. What a son of a bitch. "What is it I'm supposed to know about my dad? I haven't been to his house or talked to him and my stepmother. He has dementia, Cromwell. Maybe she took him to a hospital for care? And if everything is gone—" I held out my arms. "What am I supposed to do? I don't have magic. You took that away from me before Yule. Are you accusing me of somehow magically making them disappear with my bare hands?" I ran my fingers through my hair. "Get out. All of you."

I was juiced with something that smoldered in my very veins at that moment. I also knew if I didn't get them out of there right then, there was going to be more than just exploding water fountains. I had that same red haze in front of me; the same knot in the pit of my stomach, and the voices had become a murmur in my ears. I knew if I wanted, I could reduce each of them to ash. Little piles of gray ash I could sweep into the dirty street outside my shop walls.

Kyle placed himself between the powerful Witch and myself, his hands balled into fists. If there wasn't a magical cap on the vicinity, I knew those fists would be ignited in blue and yellow light. "You heard her. You have been asked to leave. Without express written consent by the local magistrate of the Parliament representatives in this Parish, you aren't allowed to remain once asked to leave. The only way that can be overridden is if you have legal documentation of a complaint against the property owner. Do you?"

I peeked out from behind Kyle's shoulder to get a good look at Cromwell's face. It was not an expression I ever wanted directed at me.

But to my surprise, Cromwell turned, motioned with his right hand and Fred fell to the ground. Fred left with a sneer directed toward me as he pressed a hand to his back, as did Mister Air and Emily. Miss Water didn't even look and hurried out through the door.

Cromwell stayed in front of the door and faced us. "Samantha, I look forward to your completion of the task."

Kyle said, "You did this to an innocent woman, Mr. Dryden. Sam's not guilty of anything. How about instead of trying to blame her for things, investigate why they happen and who has it out for her?"

Cromwell didn't say anything else before he turned and left the shop. The lights immediately flickered and my ears popped again. Kyle snapped his fingers and the blue and yellow lights vanished. Kyle was a good head taller than me, but not quite as tall as Ivan. He put his hands on my shoulders. "You okay? Why were you talking about a gnat? There are no gnats. I spelled all bugs out of this shop."

"It was nothing." But it wasn't. That voice was still there, but I couldn't make out words anymore. Just…buzzing. "That was a grand speech you gave in front of him and the others. You do know if you poke at a dragon it'll burn you."

"Dragons aren't real. Clerics are. And Clerics can't work in a vacuum. Trust me, my aunt knows the rules backwards and forwards. That's why she breaks them so often." He pulled me into his arms and we hugged. It was a rare moment for the two of us. We hadn't been particularly close since I took Crwys in as a partner of *Bell, Book And Candle*. "Sam, I think they suspect something. About you and Arcane. Why else tell you to go chase an Arcane artifact? And when it's all over with, they can't know about your Arcane, Sam."

"I know," I said, though my voice was muffled into his chest. I finally pulled back and put my hands on my hips as I looked down at Grey looking up at me. "If I tell them about the Arcane, and about what happened at my dad's they'll destroy me."

"Destroy you?" Jack moved in closer. "What does that mean?"

"It means they'll kill her. It would be a mercy killing since Arcane always causes…issues."

I sighed. "Just say it, Kyle. It causes madness."

"If it does, then why do you use it?" Jack asked.

I smiled at Jack before I glanced at Kyle, and then nodded to Jack. "You should brief him on what's been going on."

"I thought it was better not to. The less he knows the less anyone can torture it out of him."

"Torture?" Now the wolf dude came even closer. "No one said anything about torture."

"We don't torture," I said. "Much. I think the Faerie still torture. They like things like that."

You bet your ass they do.

I relayed Grey's comment.

"So what happens if you keep using this magic?" Jack ventured.

The computer flickered on and I walked to it, waiting to see if Ivan was remotely accessing it. And he was. I saw the browser open and a local news story about the two mutilated bodies appeared. "Looks like Ivan's been searching."

"The rumor is that Arcane Magic destroys Witches. It makes them crazy and they become destructive."

"You mean like your dad's house?" Jack's eyes widened as he looked at me with a newfound fear and respect.

"Yeah." I stroked Grey's fur as she leaned against my thigh. "Then there's no going back and the Witch Finders are set loose and your head is removed from your body." I gave Jack a half smile. "You know the old saying. Power corrupts. But absolute power corrupts even the incorruptible."

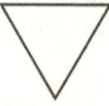

TEN

It was close to four o'clock that afternoon before Crwys got us into the morgue while Ivan and Grey stayed at the shop. It was the same one at the same hospital. But this time he got us in on a favor from the guard, who apparently owed Crwys for getting rid of two speeding violations.

The same smells as before assaulted me as the elevator doors opened and Crwys led us back to the same storage room. But this time the gurney with the latest victim was out and ready. Crwys unzipped the body bag and stepped away so Bastien and Jack could move closer. They did their sniffing the body thing while I tried to keep that Chinese food down. Crwys stood close to Kyle and I. "Where's Ivan?"

I snorted before Kyle leaned in to Crwys. "He had a date."

"A date?"

"He said he wanted to stay at the shop and work, but I'm pretty sure he's got a date somewhere else. He *is* allowed to date, Crwys." I gave him a hip-bump. Imagining Ivan actually having a girlfriend brightened my mood considerably. The weight of not knowing what was happening to me, being terrified of where that extra voice was coming from, compounded with Cromwell and his Hive asking too many questions about my dad's house…it all balled into a knot in the pit of my stomach. If I didn't watch it, I was gonna get an ulcer.

But what bothered me the most was the house. How did they know? As far as I could tell, part of whatever it was I did included altering the memories of everyone those in the house were connected to. I wasn't surprised the neighbors' memories were hazy about the house, or about George Hawthorne and his wife Pauline. Cromwell Dryden was relentless in his search for the truth within the Witch community. He was going to find out exactly what happened, and he was going to keep an eye on me. Fred was going to see to that.

"What's on your mind?" Crwys leaned in close.

"Lots of things. I'll tell you about them later."

Bastien and Jack stepped away in unison. Bastien pointed to the body. "Not *frére*."

"He's right. It's not," Jack agreed.

"Can you be a bit more specific?" Crwys moved to the gurney's edge. "Was he Lycan?"

"It's the same as the girl. It's yes and no. Like Bastien said, this guy is stuck between, just like she was. And there is a smell."

Now I ventured forward, but made sure not to look at the body. Eh…I didn't do well. I did smell Arcane, but I also looked down. This body had its face removed as well. In fact… "Crwys…can you grab the other body and wheel it out here?"

He gave me an odd look but he did as I asked. Once the two gurneys were side by side and the body bags open, my suspicion was glaringly obvious.

Kyle said it. "They were mutilated the same way."

"It looks almost identical," Bastien said. He was really getting into this by leaning down, raising his hands to measure. "How does something eat in the same way?"

"Because these bodies weren't attacked for food." I needed my *dex*. That would tell me something about what I was seeing. It might even help identify what these two people were. I still had the spell; I just didn't have the Elements to make it happen. But could I still cast the spell with just a little Arcane?

"Sam…" Kyle was watching me. "Don't."

"I have to know, and I won't be using it for any destructive purposes."

"You might not, but we've seen what that type of magic prefers."

Bastien looked at Kyle and then at me. "What is he talking about, *chérie*?"

Crwys held up his hand. "I won't let it get out of hand."

"Oh?" Kyle glared at him. "You mean like you didn't let it get of hand at her dad's house?"

"Guys," I said and snapped my fingers. "Knock it off. Something attacked these two and tore them apart in precisely the same way. I think it would help if I could identify what they were. So stand back," I looked at Crwys. "Can you contain it?"

"Yes," his eyes were red.

"*Diable*," Bastien said and crossed his arms as he stepped back.

Jack moved back as well and I caught just the hint of light surrounding Kyle's hands. Okay, so he didn't trust me all that much right now. But then again, I had destroyed all of our fountains in one blast. Still felt a bit guilty about that.

I held out my hands and drew the pentagram in the air. It wasn't a necessary gesture, but it helped me focus and feel a bit safer. For the Witch, the pentagram was a symbol of protection, as it pertained to the five Elements. But making it with Arcane Magic...what would that mean?

It appeared in the air, as usual, as I summoned the power, but instead of white it was a deep, sparkling blood red. And as I drew on the Elements, they felt as if they were there, but they weren't...*right*. It was like trying artificial sweetener right after sugar. It sweetened but there was this odd aftertaste. As I finished the spell in my mind, the pentagram split into five copies of itself just like it's supposed to as it diagnosed the two intended bodies.

The results came faster than they usually did. And they came with much, *much* more.

"Sam?" Kyle prompted.

I realized I was standing there with red pentagrams glittering all around me as I read the information. "Ah..."

Now everyone was looking at me. I could see them through the superimposed readout.

I cleared my throat. "They're both showing as human, but with mangled DNA."

Kyle and Jack looked at each other, but it was Bastien that spoke, "What does that mean?"

"They've been..." I wasn't sure how to say this. "They've been purposefully transmuted. I can see bits and parts of a spell, half sentences of a ritual, and there are symbols marked on what skin is left that I can't identity." I moved the pentagrams to the side and another paragraph of information came up. This was more than I'd ever gotten from my basic *dex*. This was like *dex* deluxe. "Both of them have a symbol on their backbones." I moved the pentagrams again and this time a reddish diagram appeared with a bull's-eye on a particular bone. "Anyone else see this?"

"I see it." Bastien moved in close to look, then he turned to the bodies. Without gloves or prep, he stuck his hands in the male and moved the skin away from the backbone. "Same here." He moved to the other body and did the same.

I concentrated on the information in front of me. "Did whatever did this to them, mark them?"

The five pentagrams spun. One of them stopped with a single word. "Transmogrification."

Then the pentagrams vanished.

Bastien left the room for a while and I hoped it was to wash his hands.

"What does that mean?" Jack asked. He was just as white and pale as I felt after watching Bastien do his work.

Crwys answered for me, and he looked worried. "It's a term used for forced shifting. These two were forced to change into what I can only assume would be wolves, and either the transmogrify didn't complete or it failed."

"You think the person who did this mutilated the bodies to hide what they did?" That was me. I'd been thinking it from the moment I saw the mutilations were the same, but I hadn't meant to say it out loud.

Bastien came back in at that moment, wiping his hands on a paper towel. He tucked the paper towel into his jacket pocket when he was done. I thought that was a smart move, to not leave anything of himself behind. Being a shifter in this day and age could be dangerous, especially a known one. And given my lack of knowledge about them, they did a good job hiding themselves. "That is what I believe, *chérie*. We heard these poor victims' cries either as they mutated, or as they died when their attacker cut them apart."

"That's a huge jump," Crwys countered. "First off, the mutilations aren't precise. The coroner already ruled the female as being attacked by a canine. The damage done to the flesh, the muscle and even the bone wasn't done by a surgeon's hands. I'll admit the similarity, and I'll go with there being someone behind this transmogrification. But as a cop I have to stick to what I can see."

Bastien shook his head. "You are a strange *diable*. You have the power to know the truth and you don't."

Now everyone looked at Crwys. He took in a deep breath and exhaled. "No, I don't, Mr. LeBlanc."

Whew...at least he didn't use that dog word again.

"I'm not what you think I am. And it's understandable your senses see me the way they do." He pulled his phone from his back pocket and moved in close to take pictures of the markings. "I'll take a closer look at these symbols. They look familiar."

"Where is Levi?" I asked.

"He's outside. Not much of a morgue guy. He's also calling his people to see if there were any other Leviathans in the area."

Well that was news. "You think this was done by a Leviathan?" And of course I thought of my aunt. But I'd been pretty sure she was miles away. And that made me remember her house was still there, sitting locked up, with my name and hers on the deed, and with a dozen or more bodies buried in the back yard.

Another one of those shit storms I didn't want opened up but I was going to have to deal with eventually.

Kyle cleared his throat after he zipped both of the body bags. "There's one thing no one here has mentioned."

"What's that?" Bastien asked.

"We could ask my aunt. She might know someone who uses transmogrify in the area. And she's really good with symbols, Crwys. She might already know what they mean."

"No," Crwys and I said in unison. I knew why I didn't want to dredge up any communication with Arden Vervain, self-appointed Witch Queen of New Orleans. She and I had been engaged in an exchange with the Obsidian Queen of Faerie, Brendi. In that exchange we'd learned key information in figuring out where the Changeling children had been kept. But Brendi had deferred her price from Arden, and that bothered me. I could be that price, since I'd already reneged on a deal with Brendi once before.

I did not want to put myself in the line of fire again. Not with the Faerie Queen owed a prize.

I could only assume Crwys didn't want to get involved with Arden for the same reasons. And Arden had been in the Magical Witch Press in the past weeks, now that she was running for the High Witch seat, the one the now deceased Mr. Higgins had filled, on the local council. She took the credit for finding those children, one of them being my former boyfriend's niece.

But it was several of Arden's coven members and I who actually pulled them from the Coyote Flame. And I took a warlock intended for her. Had I heard an apology? No. Had I received even a thank you? No.

I didn't want anything else to do with Arden. Ever.

Kyle shrugged and moved away. Jack followed him and put his hand on Kyle's shoulder. I had an *awww* moment watching them.

The door opened and Levi stepped in. He looked a little ashen from the sun as he removed his shades and stopped just inside the door. "You guys find anything?"

Crwys filled him in up to us saying we didn't want Arden's help.

"Good call," Levi folded his shades and stuck them his pocket. "Got in touch with a few kin in Atlanta. They both say there aren't any Leviathans or Revenants in New Orleans they know of. But," he held up a long, thin finger. "One of them did suggest getting a meeting with Edmund Blackwood."

"Who is that?" Crwys said.

I groaned. "He's a Ceremonial Magician. I've heard his name quite a few times. He's also a local philanthropist. Got a good reputation because Cowens don't know what he does in his spare time. Like cast spells and screw with the weather." I was tired. Like, really tired. My shoulder ached as well and I rubbed at it. I just wanted to curl up in my bed with Grey and get serious sleep.

"Why would your people want us to meet with a Ceremonial Magician?" Bastien looked genuinely confused.

Luckily, Kyle had an answer. "Transmogrification is a known Ceremonial trick. They're the ones that claim they can actually turn people into frogs, why not wolves?"

"Ah," Bastien nodded. "Then Jack and I will speak with this Magician."

"No," Crwys held out his hand. "The pack is not to get involved with police proceedings."

"You're trying to impress *chérie* with your skills," Bastien winked at me. I blushed. I mean…he *is* good looking. "Because my pack will find the answers before yours."

"First up, the New Orleans Police Department isn't my pack. And second, I think exposing your pack to anyone, local authority, Witch or any other unconventional in the area, is a bad idea. Are we clear?" Crwys put his hands on his hips. The difference in their height didn't sway either of their individual power. I had a hunch that Crwys Holliard was a lot more than met the eye. Big things always came in smaller packages. I just wished I knew what was gonna pop out of that package.

Bastien smiled and I thought I saw canine teeth. "*Oui.*"

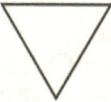

ELEVEN

Kyle somehow managed to set up a meeting with Mr. Blackwood for eight o'clock at Café du Monde. The café was one of my favorite places, and having been without their beignets for several months, I ordered three and a café au lait. I knew why the Magician picked such a well-populated place—safety in numbers—and this particular café was the most visited café in all of New Orleans.

For a Magician, their home is usually their place of power, and also where they are most vulnerable. I was pretty sure no one knew where he lived. And he would take that secret to his grave. One didn't rise to his place of power among the Magicians by blabbing secrets. And yet, giving up a secret was exactly what I wanted him to do.

The sun had set and I was starting to feel a bit of warmth on my skin. Was it the fever? Or was it the air coming from the café's heaters as we shook Mr. Blackwood's hand? I was down to twenty-four hours before I would turn. The thought of being a Lycan, forever tied to Bastien's side as his mate, was starting to look not so bad.

And *that* terrified me the most. More than being warlocked for the rest of my life.

I could feel Bastien's apprehension and discomfort being in a crowded place so Kyle and I made it easy for him and Jack and told them to wait nearby. It was going to be hard enough to get this guy to spill secrets to two Witches. Add in two Lycans?

And besides, they could both learn about the meeting if I opened the link to the pack. That door was getting harder to keep closed.

Edmund Blackwood wasn't at all what I had imagined. Then again, I didn't know where my assumption came from. Might have been Ina's tales of bad Magicians eating babies and turning bad little girls into toads. I assumed he'd be tall, gaunt and look at lot like Christopher Lee as *The Lord of the Rings'* Saruman.

Blackwood was my height, with dark skin and a very handsome face. He kept his hair close to his scalp, and it was sprinkled with gray along his temples. He wore a dark blue three-piece suit and a black trench coat, along with a matching fedora. His tie was red and in the center was a tie pin with a deep blue sapphire. Magicians coveted the sapphire. I assumed it was because it represented Water. But honestly, I had no idea. Ina sort of missed those pieces of my Witch training.

Or I was daydreaming.

Blackwood chose a table close to an exit and sat with his back to the wall. He could see the street outside but we couldn't. He removed his coat and his hat and set them in the empty fourth chair. "Well," he began in a deep voice. "It's a pleasure to meet the two of you. I've heard a lot about you both."

Great way to put Kyle and I off-guard.

"You have," Kyle said as he sipped his hot chocolate. "What have you heard?"

"That you are the nephew of Arden Vervain and an accomplished Hedge Witch. Odd to be a male born to such a feminine magic, isn't it?"

I watched Kyle's reaction. He didn't smile and he didn't blink either. He did clasp his hands together, which combined Air and Water. A breeze blew the sugar from the beignets all over the front of Blackwood's suit, making it look like a starfield.

Blackwood took in a deep breath and smiled. "Nice. Subtle. Good control and direction. Perhaps you are as gifted as I've heard." He picked up a napkin and brushed at the sugar. That motion only smeared the dots and now it looked like his suit went into warp.

"Mr. Blackwood—" I began.

"Miss Hawthorne," he interrupted and gave up trying to clean the suit. "You are the daughter of Elizabeth Hawthorne. She was a fine Witch and Tracker."

"You knew her?" I wished I'd brought Grey with me just to check this man's credibility.

"I knew *of* her. She was very instrumental in bringing quite a few rogue and transient magic users to justice. She was also a formidable Elemental. As I hear you...*were*."

Shit. He knew about the warlocking. I sipped my coffee. "Yes. I was. I soon hope to be again. But my perils and Kyle's Gifts aren't why we needed to speak with you."

"Of course not. Please," he said as he leaned back. His eyes were a light brown with very distinct pupils. I felt like those eyes were trying to see into my soul. "What can I do for you?"

I wanted to ask him why he agreed to meet with us, but I needed to get straight to the issue. "There have been two mutilated bodies found. Kyle and I were allowed to examine them and we brought in a few experts to take a look as well. The bodies were locked in mid-transformation. The experts explained they were half human and half animal. Transmogrify."

I watched his face as I spoke, careful to avoid those eyes. I thought I saw a few twitches now and then, especially when I said transmogrify.

"And you assumed a Ceremonial Magician is responsible."

Kyle took over. "We have worked with the police a few times, and discovered it's best to go to the most obvious answer and eliminate from there."

"And Ceremonial Magicians have been notorious for transmogrification." I shrugged, hoping I could make myself look non-threatening. I mean, as far as he knew I didn't have magic.

"You mean our need for turning lead into gold," Blackwood nodded. "We were alchemists at one time. A long time ago." When he brought his finger up to his lips he looked thoughtful. "There was one of my order. A woman with a long and questionable past. I took her in when she showed up on my doorstep. Back then I didn't covet my privacy the way I do now."

I took that to mean he was hiding now. "Did she try things like this? Turning people into animals?"

"She was very interested in it, yes. She insisted she knew a secret to the transforming of man into beast. But that wasn't the direction we wanted to go. A few things went missing. Ritual things. Art. Items from a few collections. And then one of our own disappeared."

Kyle and I glanced at one another.

"Disappeared?" Kyle prompted.

"She was young and in love with some boy. A Cowen. We assumed she ran off with him."

"I'm sorry but what does this have to do with—"

"Don't interrupt and listen." Blackwood sat up and clasped his hands in his lap. "Several weeks later, a member of my order found a creature in this Circe's house, the woman I took into the order. Its screams brought him into the basement and he found her notes and realized she was making a potion to turn humans into animals. And she was using Arcane to do it."

My face must have betrayed my revulsion because Blackwood pointed at me and nodded. "That was our reaction. We may see a lot of things differently, Miss Hawthorne, but on this we can both agree. The work she was doing was an abomination, and to use something as profane as Arcane Magic? This was intolerable. Once used, Arcane is uncontrollable in a warlocked Witch."

I swallowed and ignored the look Kyle shot me. "She was warlocked?"

"Oh yes. We knew that, which was why I invited her to join. She was a student of one of the more powerful of the God Mother's children. I believed she would tell me secrets, like the one she claimed she knew about transmogrification. But most of her rambling was madness. And once I learned she used Arcane, the pieces all fell into place and we banished her."

"What happened to this creature? Was it that girl that went missing?" Kyle asked.

"Oh yes. It was her. I have contacts in a DNA lab so we were able to confirm."

The irony of transmogrification and the name Circe wasn't lost on me. Neither was the fact this guy'd just reaffirmed what Crwys had told me. That warlocked Witches couldn't control Arcane. "She chose the name Circe?"

"This is why we always caution those who want to take magical names to understand the ramifications of those names. Names have power. The fact Circe turned Odysseus's men into swine was one of those ramifications. I cautioned that the name could manifest her need to dominate men or her need to make people subservient to her, which aren't bad qualities in my opinion," he smiled and it made my skin crawl. "But I never saw any of my order actually wanting to physically transform humans. There are ramifications to this on a spiritual level that I could not make her understand."

I swallowed. "I assume you never turned her over to the police?"

He shook his head and winced. "Of course not. These matters are best handled between those of us who can see."

"Well, well, well," said a male voice behind us. "Look who got to you first."

I turned and saw Crwys and Levi moving around crowded

tables. They were both dressed for business, Crwys in his jeans, shirt and leather jacket and Levi in his suit and coat. Crwys smiled at me, winked and then leaned in to kiss my lips. He pulled back just enough so our eyes met and he was frowning. If he meant to communicate something in that moment, he failed as he straightened and faced Blackwood.

"Ah…the NOPD," Blackwood looked at me. "I assume this wasn't part of our conversation?"

"Oh no, it wasn't. I didn't even know they would be here."

Levi pulled up two seats from a neighboring table and the detectives sat down. Levi held out his hand first. "I'm Detective Levi Tulose, Mr. Blackwood. This is my partner, Crwys Holliard."

Crwys reached over after Blackwood shook Levi's hand. When Blackwood's eyes widened at Crwys's touch, I worried. Was it possible that this Magician could sense by touch that Crwys wasn't human? He didn't have that reaction when he touched Levi's hand, but then Revenants weren't always that easy to detect without knowing what you were looking for. They resided in living bodies, with heartbeats, warm temperatures, and they could eat if they wanted.

Crwys pulled his hand back first and smiled. "So, you three have any interesting information on the mutilated bodies?"

Blackwood didn't answer. He was staring at Crwys a little too hard.

"Ah, we have a name to look for," Kyle said. "Mr. Blackwood, do you have her birth name?"

He nodded and tore his gaze from Crwys. "Yes. Olivia Graham. I believe she still has a house in Louisiana, or just over in Mississippi."

Yeah, I was sure this Circe kept her power base as close a secret as Blackwood.

"Detective Holliard?" Blackwood frowned at him. "Crwys is a very interesting name. It means cross, doesn't it? Welsh?"

"Yeah, that's it. You know about names?"

"I do indeed. I specialize in them. And eyes…because eyes tell us a lot of things. And you have very unusual eyes."

Crwys leaned back. "Are you hitting on me, Mr. Blackwood?"

Kyle, Levi and I watched the interchange like a ping-pong match. There was something very subtle going on here but I just didn't get what. I wasn't that sure Crwys knew either.

Blackwood placed his hat on his head, stood and slipped into his coat. "I believe our meeting is over, Miss Hawthorne. Mr. Kendrick. I hope my information proves to be of use. Please, enjoy your beignets and café au lait."

Crwys stood up fast, his chair scraping along the floor. "Mr. Blackwood, we're not done."

"Yes we are, Detective. For now." He nodded, tipped his hat to me and shoved his hands into his pockets, whistling as he left the café.

When Crwys sat down he grabbed a beignet and bit into it, getting sugar all over his face and jeans. I watched him for a few seconds, pondering his eyes. "You do have very odd eyes, Crwys."

"That's because he's an asshole," Levi said. "So that's the name you got from him?"

"Yep. Olivia Graham." I filled the two of them in on what little Blackwood said.

Crwys wiped his mouth with a napkin and drank some of my coffee. "We can run her name through the system. No address?"

"Nope."

Levi said, "We'll need to find out if this woman's legit and not someone Blackwood has a vendetta against."

"Is he known for doing that?" I looked at Levi as I took a bite of a beignet. OMG…so good!

"Yeah, he's got a hate streak as long as this county. Don't ever get on his bad side," Levi smacked Crwys's arm. "Hear that?"

"Yeah. But that guy doesn't scare me," Crwys leaned in close to me. "You're hot."

I swallowed the beignet and laughed. "You're hot too."

"No, I mean you've got a fever."

"No I don't."

"Trust me, babe. You have a fever. The transformation is starting. That means less than twenty-four hours left. We need to get this rolling. We'll run this woman's name through the system. You need to get back to your apartment."

"No," Bastien said as he and Jack joined us at the table. I hadn't sensed Bastien at all. Was it because Crwys was near? "*Ma petite* needs to stay close to me. The fever is starting and other wolves will be attracted to it."

I nearly choked on my coffee and set it down, splashing it on the table. "What? Say that again?"

"Your shift is going to attract other wolves," Bastien smiled and I didn't like it. "Like a bitch in heat."

I didn't like this at all.

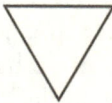

TWELVE

Ivan was at the shop, running what looked like a diagnostic on the computer. The screen was flashing up numbers and graphs and stuff that made my head hurt. His eyes were closed as he sat on his stool with his hands out on his thighs, palms up. I could see the different flashes of colors as data came and went.

He'd told me once what the colors meant to him and for the life of me I couldn't remember what he said. I kept smelling…

Bastien.

Sweet Lady this was not good!

I looked past the counter to the locked shop doors. People walked back and forth along the sidewalk, on their way to *LaFitte's* or staggering home.

Kyle filled Ivan in while I heated up left over Chinese. I'd eaten all my beignets and drank all that coffee, but I was still starving and needed tea. Something to kick-start my brain. It was actually nice not having Crwys or Bastien around. Their absence gave me time to think and try to get a bearing on what the hell was going on. While sucking in noodles, I retreated to my seldom-used office with Grey at my side. She plopped down on her oversized dog mattress in the corner while I sat at my desk. I noticed a thin layer of dust over the surface and on the mounting stack of bills I hadn't paid yet.

My phone buzzed and I worked it out of my pocket. It was Arden Vervain. Pfft. Screw that. I declined the call and tossed it on the desk. I turned to face my computer and wake it up, and I realized I forgot my password. This was telling of my lack of computer knowledge. I wasn't actually on this computer enough to remember the password. I stared at the screen saver and angrily chewed.

The screen saver flipped off and dots formed along the input line on their own and my computer was unlocked. All by itself. I realized Ivan had helped me out. I kind of wondered what it would be like to be able to actually look into the Cyber World and peer into other people's unprotected computers. Speaking of which, I eyed the camera built into the top of the screen. "Are you looking at me?"

An IM program launched and a window came to the front. **Not really**, came the letters next to an icon that looked like the letter I in a Superman logo.

"Think you can find this Olivia Graham, aka Circe?"

Not sure. I found some candidates. Kyle thinks we should ask his aunt.

"No. Tell him he'd better not call her. I don't want to go near Arden."

A few minutes passed while I ate more noodles and then I turned and opened the small fridge under the desk. I had a six-pack of Evian, two yogurts that were way past their expiration date and…I honestly wasn't sure what was in the Tupperware. It had already transmogrified into something other wordly.

My screen flickered as several windows popped up in the browser. They were local articles and business pages from five years ago. As they each showed up, the same name was apparent in bolded font.

Olivia Graham.

And in two of the articles with pictures, she was standing beside none other than—

"Holy shit!" I dropped my chopsticks.

Inamorata Devonshire.

My "aunt." The woman who raised me. I gripped the sides of the desk to steady myself as the room started wavering and my chest ached where the mark was now on fire. I didn't need a mirror to know it was sparkling a bright red.

A Leviathan made a deal with the Obsidian Queen of *Alfheim* to make my mother disappear. I was eight at the time. And from what I learned eighteen years too late, that Faerie took my mother and turned her into a paladin, a wolf of the wild hunt. And that's where she remained while my father and I believed she had died.

Enter my mother's best friend, Inamorata Devonshire. She came to my father and offered support. Moved in. And became our surrogate mom until my dad found Pauline and wanted to remarry. Then there wasn't enough room for Ina. Ina was the only mother I remembered, so I moved with her to New Orleans when I was fourteen. And here I lived with her, worked with her and admired her.

Until a few months ago, when I realized Ina was possessed by the very Leviathan that got rid of my mother. My mother's destroyer had raised me, taught me magic, knew everything there was to know about me and manipulated me into taking a human life so she could take its soul.

When the demon inside of her, the Leviathan called Dionysus, got what it wanted and it tried to drain me of blood. Luckily for me, Crwys and Grey, my mom, arrived and stopped it. But it was still out there.

And here it was, smiling in a picture with a woman who may or may not be a Ceremonial Magician responsible for two deaths, not counting the one Blackwood mentioned.

The door to my office opened and Kyle came in. "You okay? Ivan said to check on you."

"You...you saw the pictures he found?"

"Yeah. And I'm not surprised. Ina had, or has, money, Sam. It seems natural she'd be in the Society pages."

"And this woman?" I pointed to the screen. "This Olivia woman?"

Olivia in the picture was older, elegant in a slim fitting gown with perfectly coiffed golden hair. Gray strands accented the upsweep at the roots and the effect made this woman look handsome. Powerful. In both pictures, the caption called the two best friends and fellow philanthropists.

"You're going to have to realize that Ina wasn't exactly a nice person. Or the Leviathan that took her wasn't," he said as he shrugged. "Ina was also a powerful Witch, even as a Hedge Witch. I'm not surprised she attracted someone like Olivia Graham."

"You think Olivia knew she wasn't human? You think maybe she knew Ina was a Leviathan?"

Kyle shrugged again. "Who knows? Right now we need to concentrate on finding Marilla and André."

"Are those their names?" I already knew the answer to that. The pack link vibrated when Kyle spoke them.

"Yeah. Ivan's got an address. It's the last known mailing address for Olivia Graham. One of those big houses in the Garden District. It's not far from Ina's house."

"Is she there?" I set the noodles down. "I mean is Olivia at the Garden District house?"

"We're not sure. Ivan's looking into her security to find out," Kyle moved to the side of the desk. "We've got to see her tonight. Ivan said it was easy to find her, so that means Crwys and Levi will find her too."

I kept my gaze on his face. "And you're pretty sure Jack's going to look her up as well and tell Bastien."

Kyle touched his nose. "Jack's fast, but he's not as fast as Ivan."

"So you're saying we've got maybe what…an hour on them?"

Kyle nodded as he looked at my phone as the message for a voicemail showed up. He pointed to it. "You need to call her back. She said she had bad news and needed to talk to you. She's also got news on this Codex."

I glared at him. "You told her."

"She really does have a wealth of knowledge, Sam. You know that. And she told me the Codex was created by a crazy Witch to bring Arcane into the world. It's supposed to tap into the God Mother's connection and infuse it with Arcane." Kyle shook his head. "You really need to call her. She wants to talk to you."

Given what Arden had weighing on her, I assumed what she wanted to talk to me about was the Faerie Queen's payment. The fact she was calling me made me think Brendi had demanded me. And if Arden didn't deliver on that price, then Brendi had already said she'd take Arden as payment.

No one wanted to be taken by the Faerie Queen into *Alfheim*. I looked over at Grey in her bed. The current Faerie Queen likes to turn people into wolves, too. I took in a deep breath. "No. I can't help Arden this time."

"You think Brendi's told her she wants you."

"Why else would she call me with bad news?"

"Sam, she made a deal with the Faerie Queen to find those children. You owe her."

Excuse me? I stood at that moment and stared him down.

Sam, don't. Grey's voice was a soothing, cool compress on my heated temper. *He's just worried about his aunt. She's really all the family he's got that he can trust.*

Which wasn't saying a lot. So I backed down and sat on the desk. "Look, do you want me to go see Arden so she can somehow capture me and send me to *Alfheim*?"

"No. But I don't want her being taken either. You think you can get Brendi's dad to vouch for my aunt too?"

I snorted. "I doubt Brendi's dad and Arden would get along. He'd be lying if he vouched and you know how much the Faeries hate that." Truth was very important to the Faeries. They themselves couldn't lie, especially when asked a direct question. "Look, let's find the two wolves, get the unborn baby back to the pack and worry about this later."

"What if she set a deadline?"

"Kyle, *I'm* on a deadline. And I don't want to be that damn wolf's mate."

Can I? He's hot.

I rolled my eyes. "Mom!"

Sorry. Just trying to lighten the mood.

My phone went off again. Arden Vervain. I declined and blocked her number. For now.

Ivan came through the door, rubbing his eyes. They were still just a bit green. "Circe's at her house in the Garden District. She attended some fundraiser earlier in the day. I've downloaded everything onto your phone. It's all in PDFs, so you should be able to read or reference it when you want. I've added her address and her financial history. I can get her LUDs (local usage details) too if you want, in case you want to know who she's been calling."

"No, no," I held up my hand. "That's fine. I'm sure Crwys is looking into the same thing and he can do it legally."

"So are you guys going to see her tonight?"

I agreed we needed to get ahead of Bastien on this. Even with Ivan being faster, Jack would be able to find the information, so it could mean the pack would show up in the Garden District. And that would be bad.

"I can see from the look on your face you're puzzling it out. So," Ivan pointed behind him. "I'm gonna head home. Just ring me if you need anything?"

"Sure." I watched him go. I was pretty sure he was going to see his girlfriend again.

I stood up, grabbed my box of noodles and chopsticks and scooted Kyle out of my office. I asked Grey to come with me and shut the door. We walked across the break room and headed up the stairs to my apartment. Grey jumped on the couch and watched me. *I would never let Arden hand you over to anything Faerie.*

I tossed the box of noodles into the trash and sat on the couch with Grey. I hugged her tight. "I know."

Mom's memories of Ina were sketchy. She knew the name, but wasn't sure who it was. A lot of things in her past were like that, and I didn't know if that was part of the spell the Queen put on her or if eighteen years as a wolf had worn those human memories down. What she did remember was her hatred of *Alfheim* and everything in it.

I didn't know if there was a way to make her human again. Everything I consulted, from tome to Grimoire all said the one who turned her into a paladin had to be the one to turn her back. That would be Medbh, the Obsidian Queen before Brendi. And Brendi now had Medbh's essence, or soul or whatever it was, in *Alfheim*. I loved my mother but I wasn't going near another Cairn, or Faerie ring, into that realm.

Kyle came up the steps with his coat on. "You ready?"

"You think this Olivia knew what Ina was?"

He pursed his lips. "It's possible. Leviathans and Ceremonials have something in common."

"What's that?"

"Evilness," he grinned as he came into the living area and plopped onto the couch. "Let's speculate that Ina knew Olivia was Ceremonial and she was warlocked. What kind of mutual relationship could the two of them have because of that?"

"All kinds," I said as I rubbed Grey's neck and then hugged her to me. She woofed and then pulled back, put her paws on my shoulders and licked my chin before she settled down on the floor, her upper half in my lap. "Leviathans can switch bodies at will, as long as they're not fused soulless like Ina was. It might be that Ina's use of Olivia was to garner information. I would assume a Ceremonial would know Arcane."

Kyle made a rude noise. "Know of it? Sam, they crave it. Arcane is like the dark side of the force. It's an easy way to power. I've even heard *you* say how easy it is to give into the power. Look what happened last night in the shop. You broke every fountain we had on display."

"Why is that?" I prompted. "Why did I break every fountain? Why not something else? I only hit water." This hadn't been a point before but now it seemed important. Somehow. I just didn't know the how.

"To make a really long winded schooling on the Ceremonial short, let me point to the old feud with the Hammer."

"Yeah, I know. The Witches stole it from the Magicians to prevent them from using it, only to find out that no one could. Because no one could figure out how it worked."

"Except Ina," he leaned forward. "Remember? It was Ina that used your mother's athame to decipher the words. She already knew how to decipher the Hammer. How is it your mother's best friend, known only as a Hedge Witch, had been able to decipher what an entire Parliament of Witches couldn't? Where do you think Ina might have gotten that information?"

Sweet Lord and Lady! "That would mean Ina and this Olivia are still in contact."

"Maybe. From what I read, Olivia has been a bit of a recluse for the past two years. No one knows why."

I put my hand on his knee. "Let's get going. We need to go check her out ourselves."

My phone rang again and I almost automatically sent it to voicemail. Almost. I remembered I'd blocked Arden's calls so I looked at the face.

It was an unknown number. I showed it to Kyle who immediately grabbed it from me. "Jack, what's wrong?"

I dislodged Grey as I stood up and stared at him, wishing I had Ivan's ability to listen in on phone conversations. I held out my hands as Kyle jumped up.

"We'll be right there," he disconnected and handed my phone back. "Bastien did exactly what you thought he'd do. They found Olivia Graham's house and followed the leads. Now Bastien's gone into her house in the Garden District. He told Jack to stay put, but that was half an hour ago. And he just saw Crwys and Levi pull up."

"Lady Darksome…those assholes were supposed to call us." I grabbed my bag off the couch, my twin Smith & Wessons, appropriately named Lord and Lady, and my heavier leather jacket. Well, Crwys's jacket. "I'll drive. Need to swing by to pick up your gear?"

I gave Grey a quick request to stay in the shop for two reasons. First, I wanted someone watching it, and second I didn't want her even slightly involved in anything else that dealt with wolves. I couldn't handle that bitch of a captain storming into my home and taking my mom again.

Kyle shook his head as we went down the steps. "Nope. I keep a starter kit with me lately."

"Good," I said as I shut down the shop and we headed out the back to my Jeep. "Then let's roll."

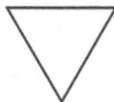

THIRTEEN

The GPS on Kyle's phone led us to a monster of a house. There were tons of monster houses in New Orleans, especially in the Garden District. But this one...I might have said it made Arden's Gypsy Gardens retreat appear small. And I knew what the square footage was in that house.

The place dwarfed the two classic antebellum homes on either side and it was literally two streets over from Ina's home. Lights were on inside and I could see Crwys's Mustang parked a few houses down. Jack greeted us after I parked, using my "park fu" to find a good, legal space across the street. Jack wore jeans, a heavy coat, no shirt and no shoes. Shivering, I got out of my Jeep wishing I had gloves as I shoved my guns into my belt at the small of my back. I had hoops stitched in some of my jeans just for this purpose, to give them a bit more stability. I liked keeping them hidden. I had a permit to carry them; I just wasn't sure where I put it. No, they didn't shoot magical bullets, but they were spelled to hit anything I shot at. This little ability wouldn't be considered legal in a shooting tournament, but it'd saved my bacon a few times.

"Jack," I said as I stared down at his dirty, bare feet. "Shoes? You got boots?"

"No. I mean yeah, I have them in the car, but it's hard for me to shift fast when my feet are in shoes," he held up his hands. "Just a quirk of mine."

I laughed, knowing how much Kyle didn't like feet. Really. He wasn't a fan of feet and preferred socks just so he didn't have to look at them. I wondered how this little idiosyncrasy would play out between them.

Kyle came around from the passenger side, his bag of herbs, ointments, tinctures and his version of gris-gris which he called spell-bags, all ready in a bag across his shoulder. "So what's going on?"

"How did you two find this place so fast?" I asked Jack.

"Bastien has friends all over the city. That's something I think you should know. Most of them are what he calls *protégé*. Those he protects for pack favors. They were able to track down who this Circe might be, gave him this address and he ordered the pack to stay alert."

"The Aces are here?" Kyle pointed to the ground.

"Yeah," I said as I felt the nudge on the pack link's door. The voices on the other side seemed agitated. Angry. Worried. Frightened and a bit lost. "They're here. The pack's lost their connection with Bastien." And so had I.

I pulled my phone from my jacket pocket and pressed the call button on Crwys's profile. It rang three times before his voicemail picked up. I waited it out and then said, "If you are in trouble, send me a flare."

Only Crwys would know what that meant. I disconnected and shoved the phone back into my pocket as I watched the house. We waited five minutes. No flare.

"He might not be able to get to his phone." Kyle wanted to sound reassuring, but I was thinking the same thing. If he were injured, or even more unbelievable, unconscious, then leaving a message on the phone would be useless.

"I've got an idea, but I need the two of you to be ready in case I…" I shrugged. "Trigger something?"

"Crap, you're going to use Arcane again?" Kyle hissed.

I turned and glared at him. "You got a better idea?" I hissed. "It's the closest I got to magic."

"Then let me do it. At least mine won't send up a red flare. Literally." Kyle moved to the back of the Jeep and opened up the door. There wasn't much space behind the second set of seats but there was enough for him to work. He set his bag down on the rubber liner, pulled out a green candle about the diameter of my wrist and maybe four inches high. He snapped his fingers and a tiny Salamander sparked a flame. I smiled at his prowess as he thanked the Fire Element and then pulled a stick of incense from a plastic wrapper.

Now here's where an Elemental Witch and a Hedge Witch differ. When I had my Elementals, I used my own essence, power, soul, pick a name, to power the spell and the Elementals were the ones that guided the intent along. They jolted my power to…I don't know. A million? I'm not a gamer so I didn't know how to rank power boosts. It was a lot. And when it was over, I would be exhausted and starving. Much like Ivan was today.

But Kyle had learned how to tap the power of the herbs, potions, tinctures and the organic and sometimes inorganic objects around him. Every potion he made, every spell he wrote, every candle he created, everything had a purpose. He used his energy to guide but he drew the power from the objects.

I pulled Jack closer as Kyle faced the ginormous house, held up the candle and traced a Water invoking pentagram in the air. It stayed there, a brilliant blue against the backdrop of the night. He set the candle on ground just beneath it, then took the burning incense stick and pierced the pentagram's center.

The middle popped like a bubble and abruptly the house looked very, very different as long as we looked through the pentagram's center.

"Holy—" Jack said a little too loud and I clamped a hand over his mouth.

Kyle spoke but his voice was little more than a whisper as he concentrated. "That's a lot of Arcane."

And it was. The entire house was on fire with it. It permeated the wood, the roots of the nearby trees and the very foundation of the place. And just past the flaming, glittering forbidden magic I could make out the outlines of six individuals. They appeared to be… "Are they having tea?"

"Looks like it," Kyle whispered. "I'm not sensing any distress. Not even an emotional spike. They're all in the front parlor."

"Wait," I pulled my hand from Jack's mouth with a warning glare and moved in closer to the pentagram. "You mind if I tweak it?"

"Let me transfer it to you. I love you, Sam, but I don't want Arcane taint."

I snorted.

Kyle knelt beneath the huge floating blue pentagram and pulled a white handled knife from inside his jacket. A Witch's working knife. I could just see the smoke from the candle as it curled up and mingled with the pentagram above. He said something under his breath and sliced the stream of smoke. The candle went out.

"Catch it," Kyle said to me and cleared his throat.

Catch it was right. The pentagram started to float away like a loose balloon. I grabbed the edge of it with my right index finger and thumb. It immediately went from blue to red. Not a fire red, but more like Arcane red. Like blood. I pulled it down and tethered it in place in front of me. What I wanted to do was see this Circe for myself. This Olivia Graham.

Of the six bodies in the front parlor, there was one that didn't reflect the red sparkling Arcane. It looked more like an outline of a void and was seated in a chair in front of a roaring fire.

"Can you tell me what's going on?" Jack sounded frightened.

"I created a window using herbs and colors of the Elements. The candle is green and the wax was made of plants and herbs with powerful Earth connections. Green is the color of Earth. The flame represents Fire, and the incense is made of Air herbs with high potency."

"The blue pentagram?"

"Communication. It's made of Water. We needed to communicate with the wood of the house so I used the other three Elements to create the window, held it in Water and pierced it with Air," Kyle paused. "It's still not making sense to you, is it?"

"No. Not really. But then, I turn into a wolf when the moon's full so sense kinda flew out the window for me a while ago. So, why is it red now?"

"Because Sam is using a different kind of magic."

"The bad magic?"

"In the wrong hands…yes."

I had to shut their conversation out as I concentrated on this void person. I repeated the *dex* spell I'd used earlier and framed it inside the pentagram, hoping the Arcane swimming about in that house wouldn't alert the owner I was probing. The spell bounced around a bit, giving me answers like Revenant, Lycan, Witch, Cowen, Ancient, Cowen—

"Ancient?"

Kyle stepped up. "What's Ancient? You mean this version of the *dex* is saying one of them is ancient? Is that a designation or a description?"

"I—I don't know. There are six people. So that's Circe, Bastien, Levi, Crwys and two more." I pursed my lips. "Maybe Circe's the Ancient?" What the hell was an Ancient?

"I'm betting she's the Witch."

I looked away and stared at him under the street lights. "You mean, she was a Witch and went Magician?"

"Not the first time it's happened. Arden could tell you some seriously scary stories about Witches who were seduced by Ceremonial

Magic. It's easier and it makes you more powerful," he snorted. "If it doesn't kill you first."

"You mean if whatever you bind into you doesn't kill you." I looked back though the window at the forms. Ceremonial Magicians have a lot of problems, the worst of them, in my opinion, was their inability to ask. If they wanted something they forced it. Which made the idea of this chick performing transmogrify all the more plausible just as Blackwood said. "I don't see any other bodies in the house. That's it."

Kyle put his hand on me. "Uh oh."

I caught the movement seconds before he touched me. It was to the side, low to the ground and just behind the fence circling the house. I moved the pentagram to see it, or to see what it was. And when I did—

Look out!

I never got a chance to shout those words out but I was thinking it when whatever it was leapt over that fence and came at us. I acted on instinct again which, in hindsight, was both good and bad. I pushed my hand through the center of the pentagram as the shadow zeroed in on me. The skin on my hand and wrist caught fire and it felt as if the window were made of real glass instead of Air and it was shredding my skin as I poked through.

I gathered every Element in every herb, in every color from that pentagram and within seconds the thing shrank and wrapped around my wrist. It burned with a flame that alternated between the Elemental colors and as the shadow made that last leap across the street and charged into the air to attack me, I focused that power on it and released.

Streams of red, blue, yellow and green shot out from my hand, encased the creature and in an instant…it was gone.

The street returned to the quiet night and there was nothing in front of us but the calm appearance of the house. I couldn't see inside of the house anymore, but the light in the parlor was out.

"What…" Kyle said but I held up a hand for him to be quiet.

The front door opened in the shadow of the street lights and a tall, feminine figure came down the steps. The gate opened and she walked, almost glided, across the street toward us. She was tall and too thin. Like rail thin. Quick, get this woman a sandwich! Her hair was white and fell in cascades over her shoulders. She wore a thigh length black dress with matching black pumps. And the face that appeared under the hair, now illuminated by the street lights above, was young.

She looked maybe sixteen. The edges of her features blurred a bit when she talked and I realized she was using glamour of some kind to hide her features.

I knew before she stopped in front of us that this was Olivia Graham, aka Circe. She had the slippery, shimmery feel of a Ceremonial Magician.

The woman with the child-like face held out her hands. "I am Circe. I'm afraid that was a dear pet of mine you just destroyed."

I stepped in front of the other two. "It attacked me."

"It was defending its home."

"We never moved from this spot. We are across the street. Not on your property," I narrowed my eyes at her. "I'd like to see Detectives Holliard and Tulose, as well as Bastien LeBlanc."

"I'm afraid I don't know those names."

"Yes you do!" Jack shouted, letting his emotions get the better of him. "I saw them go into your house!"

I turned and gave him a *Shut The Fuck Up!* glare before I turned back to Circe. She was smiling. "We know our friends are in our house. Will you let them leave?"

"For a price."

Crap. "What price?"

She smiled as she pointed at me. "You."

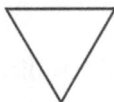

FOURTEEN

I'm not gonna deny that I suspected for a tiny second this woman might be Brendi in disguise and this was a clever ruse to save her reputation. After all, I was the only human that's ever broken a deal with any of the Faerie Queens and survived intact. But a second later I realized this lady wasn't Faerie. I wasn't sure she was sane. "Why me?"

"I know your aunt. In fact, I met you a few times when you were a child. Ina and I were very good friends at one time. We had a dream, she and I. A dream to bring Arcane into the world."

Uh...

I narrowed my eyes at her. "Ina wanted to bring Arcane into the world?"

"Of course. Because she used it. You had to have known that, Samantha. Because I can sense it within you. And it's concentrated over your heart. It's strong. You're her legacy. She always believed you could wield Arcane as well as your Gifts."

Crwys's words came back to me. *"Don't blind yourself to the possibility that his ultimate goal was to infuse you with Arcane, and then take your body. Think of the power he would have then and your soul to ride."*

Oh hell no!

Circe clapped her hands together. "I see in your face you've discovered the truth! And now you see, I have everything I need to bring Arcane into the world!"

I swallowed. "Why? And how? How...do you plan on bringing Arcane into the world?" I've learned through life that there are no coincidences. That paths cross and intertwine for a reason as Destiny sets her fickle-ass plans down.

"I think you already know, Samantha. I know Cromwell is looking for me. And I know he approached you to find this." She reached into her robes and retrieved a small, golden Codex. To most, it looked like papyrus wrapped around a golden shaft with blunted ends to keep the paper in place.

To me it looked as red as a ruby and sparkled just as bright. She had in her hand the one thing standing between me lifting the warlocking.

I reached out for it and she pulled it away. "Oh no, no, no. Ina said you're not allowed to have it."

That stopped me. "You've talked to Ina?"

"Of course. She translated the scroll before she gave it to me."

Lady Darksome! "Circe, do you or don't you have the missing pack members here? A boy and a girl?"

"Interesting change of subject, Samantha. My request stays the same. Only, you can't have the girl."

"The boy?"

"You'll have to catch him. All my transmogrify attempts failed, except for two. One of which you just destroyed, and the other," she said as she raised her shoulders and sighed. "I haven't been able to get him back yet."

"Get him back?" Kyle blurted out. "You mean there really is a monster out there?"

"There's always a monster running around out there," Circe directed her attention at me. "The decision is yours. Come with me and they all live. Or don't and everyone dies."

The door to the house opened and another tall young lady ran out. She wore a similar black dress and brandished a big knife.

Circe looked irritated when she looked at the girl. "Why are you interrupting me?"

"My Lady!" The girl was out of breath and I noticed several cuts on her arms, as well as her face. Her hair was also mussed. "The potion's not working on any of them!"

Oh no. She gave all three of them one of her potions. All I could think about was Crwys being torn apart as some potion turned him into half a wolf.

Wait…she just said it wasn't working on any of them.

Circe lowered her arms. "That can't be right!"

"Nothing's happening. My Lady—"

Circe struck the girl hard across the face. She fell to the asphalt in a heap. "And you left them alone?"

Uh oh.

I looked around the neighborhood at the houses. If Bastien was out of that house, I was pretty sure he was going to call the Aces if Jack hadn't already. As for Levi and Crwys? I wasn't sure what the hell they'd do. Given Levi had been in the sun all day and was probably hungry, and when Crwys got mad he set people on fire, I figured we should be ready for anything.

Circe pointed at me. "You can have the rest, but the girl and her baby are mine!"

I shook my head. This woman was certifiably bat-shit crazy.

The front doors on all the houses on the street flung open at once. Black robed figures came running out of each front door, six doors in all. It looked like black ants marching out of holes in the walls, only sped up. These guys were running.

Kyle ducked behind the Jeep again and I heard his snap and the tiny cry of a Salamander ready for war. The sound tore at my heart as I missed my own Salamander. All of my Elementals. I just wasn't whole without them. A miasma of colorful pentagrams filled the air around us, creating a sphere that encased Kyle, Jack, the Jeep and I. Whatever these things were that were coming out of the houses, they were completely robed, hooded and gloved. From what I could see through the rainbow of pentagrams there wasn't a single piece of flesh visible on any of them.

"Sam! I need power!"

"You sure?" I had my weapons out, safeties off and pointed at the sky. "You want that taint?"

"Just juice the ward."

I was going to oblige him when one of the robed things broke through the pentagram on my right. I fired once at it and the bullet slammed into its head. It vanished and the bullet hit the asphalt with a ping.

-*You'll need more to defeat these creatures.*-

I ignored the voice and shot at another one as it broke through close to Kyle.

"Sam!"

"Hold on!" But I couldn't concentrate on sending any kind of power into the shield while I was shooting at black robed zombie things. My bullets were making them disappear, but they were still coming out of the doors. I needed to know what they were in order to actually fight them.

"*Sam!*"

That wasn't Kyle that time. I shot another black robed dude. "Crwys? You okay?"

It was a few seconds before he answered. He was somewhere outside the sphere in the dark. I could hear him but I couldn't see him. "I will be. What do you need me to do?"

I hit two more. I was going to run out of bullets. "I need you to get rid of these things before they get inside the pentagrams. I need a minute."

"Will do."

Almost immediately, I saw a few of them flame out of existence. I had no idea who else could see that, but I didn't care. I tossed my guns into the back of my Jeep and conjured the *dex*. This time I focused on the black robes. What I got back was...odd.

"Sam?" That was Kyle this time.

I looked at him. Kyle was standing in the center of the pentagram sphere, holding the incense in one hand and the lit candle in the other. He was acting as a grounding line and feeding power directly from the Earth to the wards. But that wasn't going to last forever. The power running through Kyle was going to burn him up. Jack stood beside Kyle, looking at the Hedge Witch as if he were a super hero. "Kyle, these things are registering as something weird."

"Tell me!"

"The *dex* is saying smoke, but it's also got all four Elements and a bit of the fifth."

Kyle looked at me. "Illusion. But it's being siphoned off the people in the houses. She's using an old Ceremonial trick. Arden calls it smoke and mirrors."

I saw a few more of the black robes poof off in flame. "But Crwys is able to ignite them."

"Yeah, I see that. But he needs to stop. He's also igniting innocent people's dreams."

"Seriously?"

Kyle took in a deep breath. He was starting to shake as he held the sphere around us. "She's using the dreams and essence of the neighbors, and every time he ignites one he's probably killing brain cells in whomever's head that particular robed guy came from. She's the one controlling the shapes and directing them, but they're giving her the power. One of the Magician's best tricks is illusion."

"So how do I stop them?"

"You can't, but I can. You're going to have to take my place."

Uh. What?

He gestured me to him with a nod. "Hold up your hands and use that magic of yours to form a sphere around us. Just close your eyes and trace the same outline, same pattern. If you waver and make a gap, one of them can get in and Crwys won't be able to make it burn."

No pressure there. I stood behind him and held out my hands to match his. Then I cupped my hand beneath his so that he could slip his hand away and I'd still be holding the candle. Then we did the same thing with the incense, but before he stepped away, I closed my eyes and called up the power like I would normally. It came fast and with a presence this time, making the mark on my chest burn.

"That's it! Just keep it there. Give me a minute."

I opened my eyes to see the pentagrams had all turned a sparkling red. All of them. I could feel the sphere as it curved over us and then sliced into the ground beneath us. I poured power into it as the robes beat against the edges of the Arcane power.

I noticed something else.

Every time they struck the sphere, they grew a little. Some were bigger than others. And growing. "Uh…Kyle?"

"I know. I see what's happening. They're feeding off it now. Just…hang on."

I glanced back to see he'd dumped everything out of his bag into the back of my Jeep. He set up a small cauldron, poured sand out of a bag into it and then set in three briquettes. I heard someone scream and then the baying of wolves.

The Aces had arrived.

Kyle dumped a whole bag of something onto the briquettes. I was about to tell him he hadn't lit them when he stepped back, grabbed a small mirror out of his bag and then pointed at the cauldron. The briquettes ignited and the incense heaped on top exploded.

Suddenly, the mirror in his hand was multiplied by a hundred if not more. In front of every black robe a mirror appeared. The robe screamed and vanished. I watched as they vanished in batches through the smoke created from the exploding incense.

Sensing no more attacks on the sphere, I let it go and the thing disappeared in a huge cloud of sparkling red glitter. I still held the incense and candle in my hands and turned to give Kyle a thumbs up. That's when something very heavy and moving very fast knocked me on my ass. I went tumbling ass over head and came up on my front. Something grabbed me at my hips, hauled me up and threw me down again. I bit my lip and my tongue as my chin struck the sidewalk. The thing picked me up and threw me into the wrought iron fence of the neighbor's yard. My head slammed backwards against the poles and I saw stars as I slipped down and rolled back onto the sidewalk.

I could see Kyle grabbing my guns from the back of the Jeep right as brilliant warmth injected itself between me and whatever it was that was beating the shit out of me.

The need to get away rolled me over onto my side as I tried to see what was happening. I could make out a hazy Crwys, his arms out at his sides and his hands on fire, as he wrestled with what looked like Big Foot. The thing towered over Crwys, and I saw something else I'd never seen before.

Blood. Crwys wasn't wearing his jacket, just a t-shirt. The scarlet blood stuck out against the white cotton as it trickled down Crwys's back and over his arms. I cried out when I realized the thing had taken a chunk out of his neck. I thought I saw bone but I couldn't be sure. They came together again and this time Crwys ignited the monster's fur.

Kyle came from the right side where my Jeep was parked and raised both of the guns, aiming at the creature. Good. The spells on them would make sure he hit that son of a bitch.

But Jack suddenly came up and grabbed the guns out of his hand. One of them fired but I didn't know where the bullet went.

"No! You can't shoot him!"

Crwys cried out in pain as the thing lifted him up and bit into his side. I could hear the rip and tear of bone and flesh as the monster ripped out a chunk and pushed Crwys past me to the fence. I screamed for him and tried to tell Kyle to shoot it.

Another blur of fur appeared, this one not as big but deep, deep red. Bastien wasn't a full wolf, but more of some half-formed wolf-man, and managed to wrap his arms around the monster as it tried to get to Crwys. I yelled again, or I thought I did, as I watched Bastien pick the monster up and toss him away. With a yellow fiery look at me, the big red wolf-man lunged after the monster.

I moved, a little, enough to see Crwys's boots to my right. They weren't moving. He wasn't moving. I turned to tell Kyle to call for an ambulance.

But Kyle wasn't there. Neither was Jack.

My guns lay on the asphalt by the back of my Jeep.

And as the night came in like a descending angel, I heard the scream of something dying.

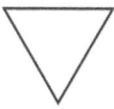

FIFTEEN

Everything *hurt*.

It hurt to breathe, to move, to swallow and to think. I was one big bruise.

"*Shugah*, you need to open those eyes up. We got a lot to do today."

And somehow my aunt had become some southern-speaking woman. Wait, that wasn't Ina's voice. I knew that voice. And I groaned out loud when I opened my eyes to see Arden Vervain staring down at me. Her dark hair was pulled back from her face in a smart ponytail and her usual smirk had been replaced by thin lips. "Finally. You do realize you've been asleep for nine hours?"

Nine hours?!

I sat up fast, and went back down just as fast as the room and bed spun underneath me. I actually moaned my head hurt so badly. After several minutes of deep breathing, I took a longer look at where I was. It was a bed, but it wasn't a hospital bed and it wasn't my bed. This one had a gold canopy hanging over me, with a large gold tassel in the center. I turned my head, slowly, and looked around the room. It looked like a bordello, with burgundy walls, white and gold Victorian furniture and a three-panel mirror on the far side of the bed. The sheets were soft—had to be four-hundred thread count. And I was wearing—

What the hell was I wearing?

It was white and soft and covered most of me. This time when I tried to sit up, Arden leaned forward and put a hand between my shoulder blades to push me forward and prop me up. Once the room stopped spinning I looked at her. "Nine hours?"

"Mmhm. I'm afraid the girls and I arrived about ten minutes too late."

"You arrived too late? How did you know—" And then I remembered Kyle's text message. "He texted you."

"Yes, he did. And it was a good thing. You have no idea what you're up against with Circe."

"She doesn't scare me."

Arden sat back and I was able to support myself sitting up.

I was covered in bandages as well as bruises. "Wait…you were calling me. What did you want?"

Arden's expression shifted a few times, from what I interpreted as surprise, then sadness and then resignation. "It was nothing. Nothing you really could have helped me with. It's all taken care of now."

Her words stuck with me because they were beyond ominous. I figured she'd already made the deal with Brendi to deliver me. I just had to get the hell out of here and be on my guard until I did.

My head really hurt. I put a hand to the back of it and felt something crusty.

"Stop that," Arden said and pulled my hand back. "You used to have six stitches back there, and two over your eye. But they mysteriously healed in the span of several hours. You've also got one hell of a concussion. I bet you don't even remember me coming in here, interrupting my night just to make sure you woke up every hour, do you? You also have this pesky fever that won't break."

I could feel the fever. I could also sense the door I'd shut against the pack's link was battered now and staying shut by sheer will. I didn't have much longer before the transformation would start. "I had stitches and they healed?" How was that possible?

"Yes. I'm willing to bet it's got something to do with that wolf bite on your shoulder."

Crap. She saw that. "Please tell me you weren't the one to stitch me up."

"Two of the best surgeons in New Orleans and a nurse are part of my coven, Samantha. They took care of you. Now, about that bite—"

"No. Not talking about that right now. But thank you for the care. Where's Kyle?" If he was here, we both needed to get out. Now. Before I became Faerie fodder.

Something in Arden's face worried me. It was probably the pinch between her brows. "Sam—"

"Arden," I matched her tone. "Where is Kyle?"

"We're not sure. We think Circe might have taken Kyle and his new beau. I ah...I haven't been able to find him. I can't even scry for him. It keeps coming up blank."

I felt as if someone had knocked the wind out of me. She took Kyle? I pushed myself up further and looked around. "Where are my clothes?"

"I'm afraid they're ruined."

"Then get out of my way. I'll go dressed in this nightgown to find Kyle if I have to."

That's when I discovered just how strong Arden really was. She was a petite woman with slight shoulders and I assumed barely weighed a hundred and ten pounds dripping wet. This tiny woman grabbed my upper arm, squeezed hard, which got my attention and woman-handled me back down onto the bed. When she let go there was a tiny red handprint on my upper arm. Looked like a hobbit tried to take me down.

Then she put a long, blue-lacquered finger in my face. "You need to stop and listen to me for once, Samantha Hawthorne. Kyle is my nephew. *My* kin. And even I'm not dumb enough to go charging out there into the world with no intel or plan. I want him back, and trust me, the last person in the world I would ever want to have any of my family in her possession is Olivia Graham."

Something in Arden's voice frightened me. Not like a quick scare, but a deep, anxious fear. "How do you know her?"

My host sat back down on the bed beside me and clasped her hands together. "Olivia is the poster child for Arcane possession, Sam. She was an Elemental Witch, just like you. Just like your mother. And she was one of the most powerful in the country. She knew your mother, which is how she knew Inamorata."

I swallowed but didn't say anything.

"Olivia fell in love about the same time your mother met George. Her love was also Cowen, but accepting of what she was. He supported her, helped build her business of body oils and she opened several chain stores along the west coast. Quite successful. I won't mention the name because it's not important. But in the middle of that success, her husband strayed from her. I don't think it was because he didn't love her, but because she put so much energy into her stores and making money that she neglected him. So he found someone new and fell in love again. Only this was a Cowen and not a Witch.

"I don't know how Olivia found out about the relationship.

What I do know about is the aftermath. About the time your mother disappeared is when I got the news about Olivia. She'd been arrested in connection with the disappearance of a young school teacher in California. There was a trial, but Olivia was acquitted because there just wasn't any real physical evidence linking her to the young woman's disappearance other than cat hairs they found in Olivia's home. The defense argued Olivia's husband was in a known affair with this young teacher and she had been in their house several times so the hairs could have been transferred.

"And then they started looking at the ex-husband after Olivia divorced him. I thought it was weird they waited to charge him with her disappearance a day after the divorce was final. He was convicted and sentenced to life in prison without parole. And Olivia…" Arden shrugged. "She never recovered from that. She sold the business, moved back to Louisiana and bought the house near Ina's. Olivia had a big dog at the time. It went with her everywhere and obeyed her every word, even when she taught it to kill."

"Did she have something to do with that girl's disappearance?"

Arden focused on me. "Sam, the dog was the girl. She's successfully transmogrified that girl into an obedient dog and she'd used Arcane to do it."

My jaw dropped.

"We, as in the Elders in the southeast, didn't realize what she was doing until it was too late. Too late being two years ago. One of her housekeepers reported her activities to a Hive and they investigated. But by that time she'd already lost herself to Arcane. Dryden didn't know this and he warlocked her as punishment for what she'd done to that girl. He was the only Witch strong enough to do it from a distance. Until last night, no one had heard from her since. I assumed the warlocking killed her at the time. Apparently she found Edmund Blackwood and joined his order of Magicians. But even he kicked her to the curb. Hard to believe anyone is bad enough that Blackwood wouldn't keep them."

I played last night's events in my head. The darkness and the thousands of black robes coming out of the neighbors' houses. "Did you see what she did? Last night?"

"Yes. That was Arcane." Arden said this last part with a distant look on her face. "She and Ina were friends for a while. Did you know that? I didn't approve of them together which…well," she shrugged and refocused on me. "Did you see Olivia's face?"

I sensed sadness from Arden. Not something I was accustomed too. I also assumed the three women were close friends at once, and then Arcane was what came between them.

And that Ina wasn't really human anymore.

"Yeah. But I couldn't *see* her, you know what I mean? She was blurred. The edges of her face weren't well defined."

"Ah. Then the darkness has marked her and she's hiding it," Arden pursed her lips.

"Marked her?"

"Yes. Arcane Magic behaves like a...like a parasite. It infests the body, the mind and the soul. And when it's called enough, when it's used in a powerful spell, it manifests into a single place in the body, making a mark. Most marks are on the inside, which makes the Arcane Witches hardest to find. But I'd heard Olivia's mark was on her face."

I almost put my hand to my chest where my own mark had started. Had she not seen it? She'd seen the wolf bite, but not the mark?

Arden continued. "I have a suspicion the bodies the cops found are a direct result from Olivia's experiments. If they don't stop her, she'll evade the cops again."

Cops. Crwys!

I sat forward and slapped my hands on the mattress, palms down. "Crwys! What happened to him? I saw that monster; the one that attacked me and it looked like it really hurt him. He wasn't moving."

I didn't like the expression that passed over her face. "Yes, it hurt him. But my people couldn't get to him. The Vampire he runs with wouldn't let us near him. He took Crwys Holliard away. We're not sure where they are or if Crwys survived. The captain has called your cell phone several times."

Fuck her. I didn't plan on helping that harridan again. I somehow knew Crwys was alive. If Levi took Crwys away, and wouldn't let Arden near him, I assumed he did it to protect Crwys because he couldn't protect himself. I also knew Revenants' blood had healing qualities to it. But...if humans drank Revenants' blood it turned them into Ghouls. If Crwys drank it...what would it do? I was pretty sure Levi knew what Crwys was, he just wasn't telling me. And that made me think it was something *really* bad.

I had to have faith that when Crwys was better, he would come to me. Or Levi would bring me news. They both knew a connection had formed between Crwys and I during our whirlwind romance ten months ago. And that connection had never faded. Which was how I knew he was still alive.

"She has a Codex."

"I know about it. It's an old artifact. And I know Cromwell's very eager to find it," Arden said.

"He told me to find it. If I do, he'll lift the warlock."

Arden's expression shifted. She looked irritated. "What? Why is he holding that warlock over your head? You were cleared. You know you have the right to a Tribunal. I can represent you."

"Before I saw Olivia had it, I might have taken you up on that. But I think getting it away from her is more important. If I succeed and he still doesn't remove it, I'll give you a call." I tried to smile, but I was worried now. Seeing the Codex had been a bit of a relief. There was my salvation. Arden would help get Kyle back and I knew she'd use her resources to do it. But I would still have the mark on my chest and the Arcane would be there.

"Sam?"

"What about Bastien? The Alpha?"

"He was wounded, but I'll let him tell you his story as soon as he returns."

"Returns? Is he out looking for Kyle and Jack?"

"No," Arden's expression changed again. I'd love to play poker with this woman. She'd be an easy mark. "He's out taking care of family business. But he'll be back so we can make plans."

"Plans...you mean to rescue Kyle?"

"Yes," she stood and stepped away. "Rest. It's seven in the morning. When the Alpha returns, we'll meet." And she left, closing the door behind her.

I leaned back into the pillows and stared at the tassel floating above me. My life had become a never-ending maelstrom of dramatic events. And this time I couldn't figure out where I'd stepped in it. I think on this occasion it stepped on me. But either way, I'd made a promise to myself years ago that when I set up my shop and gathered those closest to me, I would use my power to help people, Cowen and Witch alike. And so far we'd been...marginally successful.

I put my hand to my chest and felt the mark, now it felt hard like scar tissue. I looked down, my chin on my chest so I could see it. When that didn't work, I got up, slowly, and found a bathroom just off the bedroom. Clawfoot tub, double vanity with gold fixtures, two medicine cabinets, a robe and a stack of towels. I also found clothing hanging behind the door. They were my size, but they weren't exactly my style. I liked tight fitting jeans, a t-shirt, a jacket and boots.

There were boots all right. Low heeled black boots that looked like they came up to my knees. The clothing consisted of several layers of skirts, a tight small top and jacket, all black. This was Arden's style. The feel of the fabric alone told me they were expensive.

Looking in the mirror, I ignored the pale, dark haired chick with the shadows under her eyes and focused on my chest as I pulled the gown away. The symbol really was a mass of scar tissue now. In fact it didn't really look like the symbol anymore and more like a healing gunshot wound. I pressed on it with my fingers. It didn't hurt but it wasn't pleasant to look at. Crap, was it trying to heal now and whatever was there wasn't letting it?

I experimented with the power to see if the symbol still lit up by holding up my right hand to form what I would normally call on a Salamander to do. A ball of sparkling red glitter flame appeared. The scar didn't light up. It didn't even get hot. And there wasn't that creepy voice in the back of my head.

Was there some weird difference in how I used the power? Creating the *dex* at the morgue, using my guns, and just making a fireball…nothing happened. But when I popped all those fountains and when I engaged with the sphere of protection Kyle had built, I'd felt the power differently. It had been harder to control, like I was a piece of gauze in front of a raging river, tasked with the keeping the river from flooding the town.

Or that's how it felt. I'd lost that battle in the shop when Prescott took Grey. And I was pretty sure I'd have lost it if I'd seen Circe taking Kyle and Jack.

Practical verses emotional? Was that it?

Dismissing the fireball I went back into the room and looked for my things. I did find my phone on a chest of drawers. It had maybe twenty percent charge on it but it might help me Google a few questions. My eyes felt hot when I closed them and my joints ached. I definitely had a fever. And I felt a weird anxiety knowing Bastien wasn't close by.

Nope. No signal. I always forgot Arden's houses were like that. No signal in or out. But then, electromagnetic fields and magic have never gotten along.

"Sam!"

The voice coming through the phone's speakers scared the crap out of me so I dropped it. Luckily it had a good case and it hit thick carpet. I stared down at it and realized I'd nearly jumped up on the bed.

"Hey, where did you go?"

That was Ivan's voice!

I knelt on the floor by the phone and looked at the screen. There was no picture so I held the microphone end to my mouth. "Can you hear me?"

"Wow…hell yes. It's good to hear you."

"How come I can't see you?"

"Because video will use more power and your phone's down to nearly nothing."

I stared at the phone. "How is it you're doing this?"

"Do you really want me to go into the Cyber physics?"

No. Just thinking about that made my head hurt. "Where are you?"

"I'm at the shop. Where are you? I've been trying to find somebody. I came in to open and found Grey shut up in your apartment, barking, and you know I don't speak dog—" I heard Grey *woof*. "Sorry. Wolf. But no one is answering their phone. And get this…Captain Prescott's been calling. I called her back and apparently Crwys and Levi were supposed to attend a briefing last night and didn't show. They're not answering either."

I wasn't sure where to start first. I was sure we didn't have enough power in my phone for me to tell him everything. "Hold on." I brought the phone with me as I got up and went to a window. I was pretty sure I was at Arden's home in the Garden District given the impromptu battle last night had happened in the same subdivision.

But what I saw outside weren't the streets of the Garden District.

I saw endless trees; many of them covered in Spanish moss. Cars littered a dirt parking lot below and to the left was an elegant garden with a working fountain.

"Sam?"

I put the phone back up to my lips. "Sorry. I had to check where I was."

"Where is that?"

"Gypsy Gardens." Arden's plantation in the swamp. How in the hell did I get out here?

The door to my room opened and Arden peeked in. She looked at the bed and then spotted me by the window. "The Alpha's back. I'd hoped you could get more sleep, but he's ready to fight and we don't want him running off on his own." She looked at the phone and smiled. "Tell your friend to come while you get a shower. We're going to need all the help we can get." She left the room.

"Ivan, can you get out here?"

"You sure you want me out there?"

"Yeah. It think given the circumstances it's not going to matter right now. And bring Grey. I need her."

"We'll be there in an hour."

I tossed the phone on the bed and looked out at the swamp for a few more minutes before I closed my eyes and thought of Crwys. I blew him a kiss before I turned and headed back to that luxurious bathroom.

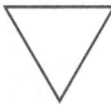

SIXTEEN

Bastien looked great for someone who just went several rounds with a monster. His red hair was pulled back in a ponytail and he wore a suit, which looked expensive, that was specifically tailored for his physique. I found him standing by the sliding glass doors looking out over a clover shaped pool. He had a mug in his left hand, a solemn expression on his handsome face. I could smell the chicory as I approached.

Either he heard me or smelled me, because he turned and stared at me as I approached. The stare was unnerving, especially under his golden gaze, so I stopped and looked down at myself. "What?"

"*Chérie*," he said and then cleared his throat. *"Trés belle."*

I blushed. I hated that I blushed. But I continued my walk toward him, the heels of my boots clacking on the hardwood floor. "Thank you. This isn't what I'm used to wearing."

"You should wear it more often," Bastien set the mug down on a nearby side table and took my hand in his. His skin was warm, not as high a temperature as Crwys's always was, but it felt good. "Perhaps the detective wouldn't leave you alone so much." He leaned in to sniff and squeezed my hand. "The fever's started."

I took my hand back. "Yes." I felt torn at that moment. Every nerve in my body tingled standing this close to him. I had fantasy thoughts of doing naughty things and blushed from them.

"You and the cop are together?"

"I don't know."

"So, you're not a couple?"

There was hesitation in my voice. "I don't know. We dated just under a year ago. It was fast and furious and our magic…connected. But there's not been anything solid since."

"Then perhaps I have a chance?"

Awkward. I didn't want to go down that rabbit hole so I clasped my hands behind me. "Will you give me the antidote?"

He hesitated. "*Chérie…*"

I knew in that one word he wasn't going to go back on his vow. He wouldn't free me from the bite until he had his people. "I see. And if she's already changed them? Transmogrified them into one of those monsters?"

"Then we're dealing with events beyond your control. I will not let you change."

That made me feel a little better. "So, why the suit?"

His face sobered and he looked out the window again. "We buried *mon frére* at dawn."

"Your brother? You found him?"

"*Chérie*, it was he who attacked last night."

I took a step back. "What?" I had very good memories of the thing that knocked me on my ass and then proceeded to slam me repeatedly into unmoving objects. And that wasn't a Lycan. Not from what I'd see of the Aces. "That's…that's not possible. How was that your brother?"

"Circe," Arden said as she joined us by the doors.

Her brows rose high on her forehead and her lips pulled to the left in a knowing smirk. "Mmm-*mmm!* I can pick clothes, can't I? Sam, if you'd wear things like this more often instead of keeping up with that dismal tough girl persona you've got going on, you'd grab a lot better men than Detective Holliard."

"I would agree," Bastien said.

And now we're heading into the weeds. "Ah…look, I obviously missed something while unconscious. Like getting out here into the swamp and that monster being your brother. You two care to fill me in?"

Arden put the back of her hand against my cheek, and then placed it on my forehead. "You still have a fever. This is no good. Let's go into my private parlor," Arden suggested and led us from the doors down the hall to a door on the other side of a bookshelf. From the other end of the hall this door wouldn't be visible. I wouldn't have known this room was there.

It was small, intimate, with a wood burning fireplace, two facing sofas, a coffee table and tea service as well as an antique roll-top desk to the right. The walls were painted soft blue and the furniture was more modern than the rest of the house. I sat on one sofa, Bastien sat beside me and Arden took the sofa facing us.

"The tea is English breakfast and it's hot. There's cream, milk, clotted cream, sugar, sugar substitute, honey, whatever you could possibly want. Samantha, *shugah*, there's some roast beef sandwiches under that dome. They're the best, and chips with it. You need to eat. Bastien's already cleaned out half of my kitchen," she smiled at him. "And charmed all the kitchen staff."

I fixed myself a cup of tea and dove into one of the sandwiches. She was right. Best thing I'd ever tasted. The beef was perfectly cooked, the cheese was asiago and the bun was toasted with butter. I nearly groaned aloud at the taste of the creamy horseradish sauce and mustard.

"Bastien, what happened? How did you three end up in Olivia Graham's house?"

He shrugged. "I don't know. I told Jack to stay in the car and I approached the door. The next thing I remembered was seeing the two detectives sitting in the front room. I was in a chair and we were drinking tea."

"Tea?" I made a face. "You don't remember Crwys or Levi coming in the door?"

"No. I awoke because I heard *mon frère* nearby. Crwys stood up and staggered to the window, he cursed in some language I've never heard and ran out the door. When I could stand without falling, I ran after him."

"Circe said she gave you her potion. I assume the same potion she used to create the two bodies we found."

"*Oui*. But how would that potion effect creatures such as us?" He winked. "It made me sick to my stomach and disengaged my mind."

It was an interesting way to say the potion knocked him out. I assumed whatever it was she'd given him wasn't the same as what she'd given his brother, or Bastien would be a monster as well. With Levi, I assumed his demon, Ashur, protected him from the potion's properties. So what prevented Crwys from changing?

Arden spoke. "I got Kyle's text and rounded up the coven, as many members as I knew who had had any kind of interaction with Circe. We got there just as Bastien's pack did, and having worked with the Aces in the past, my group and his corralled the spectres closer to you, especially once I saw what Kyle was about to do. I knew in order for it to work, they were all going to have to be within the sphere of his power, which normally isn't that large. But with your help, using magic you should not be able to use, the spectres were showing themselves."

"My pack and I were just shifting back when something came from behind the Magician's house. We all sensed it was one of us, but somehow changed. And Jack knew it was *mon frère* before I did. But he was changed, *chérie*, altered beyond anything I had ever seen. Like the bodies we saw in the morgue, but much, much larger."

I held a mug of tea in one hand and a half-eaten sandwich in the other. "What happened to him?"

"Circe happened to him," Arden said. "Apparently since her disappearance, she's been working on perfecting another potion like the one she used on her former husband's lover."

"Did she lose the original potion?"

"Who knows? It might have been something she mixed with inspiration. Whatever it was, it wasn't written down and she's been trying to make it work. She's been using Lycan blood, their pituitary glands, their brains, any part of them she can take to mix those potions."

"We've had many disappearances over the past two years," Bastien said. "But we never suspected this was happening to them. The night *mon frère* and Marilla ran off, thinking to help one of our kind—they had no idea what would happen to them. Why would anyone make a potion to change another into an animal?"

"She's crazy. But the potion didn't really work," I put the sandwich down. "We saw that in the morgue."

Arden poured herself a cup of tea. "She used one of her semi-successful experiments to reap what she needed from the body. The teeth and pituitary gland, which is why the face and throat were missing. A closer look would have shown the brain gone as well. She probably took the liver and other organs too."

I rubbed at my chin. "How do you know this?"

Bastian answered. "Because I saw it in *mon frère's* mind before I killed him."

Lady Darksome…I stared at him with complete understanding of his mood now. Of what happened after I passed out. "I'm so sorry, Bastien."

"*Non*. It was the right thing. He was in so much pain from what she did to him. She caught him and Marilla and forced the potion on him. You killed the first one, the one that mutilated the bodies and took what she needed. *Frère* attacked the two in the morgue because he sensed that magic again, the same magic we sensed before he was taken."

"Oh hell…that's why he used me as a chew toy."

"*Oui*. And when the detective tried to protect you, the two fought," Bastien sat forward. "He may be a puppy, but he's a brave one. He tried to save you."

I remembered that much. I needed to find out if Crwys was all right, I didn't think I had Levi's number. "I wish I knew how he was. Where he was."

"He was badly hurt. Miss Vervain told you the *homme mort* took the detective? I have no idea where they are," he nodded to Arden. "We have been trying to find him."

"I don't know. I don't even know where either of them live." I was shaking. I knew it was a combination of information overload, use of magic, injuries and lack of food. And full moon fever. Oy. I sipped my tea.

"So what does Crwys think of your bond with Bastien?"

And abruptly choked on the tea. That wasn't a question I expected Arden to ask. But it did make sense she would ask it because she saw the bite mark on my shoulder while I was unconscious and drooling in bed.

"The bond was necessary so *ma petite* could understand us," Bastien beamed.

I tried to hide in the cushions.

"Uh huh. You do know she's started the fever. You've got about ten hours before it's too late to give her the antidote."

My cup, tea and saucer ended up on the carpet. I grabbed the seat of the couch. "Ten hours? I thought I had longer than that," I looked at Bastien. "You said I had forty-eight hours!"

"It usually takes forty-eight hours for the venom to make the transformation. But once the fever starts, it's going to get harder for you to be up and moving," Arden glanced at Bastien. "He didn't tell you that, did he?"

"No."

Bastien held out his hands. "I thought we would have found them by now."

I was on my feet. "If I've only got ten hours, then we've got to find them. Now!"

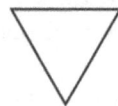

SEVENTEEN

I was ready to start calling out orders when someone knocked on the door.

Arden answered and I checked my phone. I had less than twenty percent battery but I did have a few bars so I tried Crwys's number. It went straight to voicemail.

"Hey, it's Sam. Look, I'm at Arden's and I'm worried about you. Could you or Levi please call me?" That's as much as I got out before the connection ended with a series of beeps. Out of power. Dammit.

"Sam," Arden said as she turned from the door. "You have company."

Grey threaded her way between Arden and the door and jumped up on the couch where I was standing. I could hear my mom's voice in my head, scolding me for taking chances and locking her up in the apartment. I quietly reassured her I was fine. I didn't know if Arden knew the wolf's relationship to me, other than her being my familiar. I'd lost track of what the damn woman knew and didn't know. Most of which didn't come from me. I really loved Kyle. He was my best friend. But damn, the boy needed to not be so forthcoming with his aunt about our business.

Ivan appeared at the door. He wore a concerned expression across his exotic features, but broke into a smile when he saw me. Arden moved from the door and took her seat again as Ivan closed the door and after looking around, sat down the other end of Arden's sofa. He looked good, well rested and just showered. His thick dark hair hugged his face but stuck up at the crown. Dressed in dark jeans, Vans, a Club Hell t-shirt and navy hoodie, he looked…normal.

Given the situation, I threw caution to the wind and decided to improvise. "Ivan, can you get a signal here?"

He caught on fast and pulled a tablet out of his backpack. After turning it on, he swiped the surface a few times with his fingers. "Yep. It's not the greatest signal but it's doable."

Arden's interest was peaked. "How is it he can access the Internet in this house, surrounded by so much magical energy?"

Ivan and I looked at each other and I winked. "It's because that's one of his Dianic Gifts. It's an odd Gift, to say the least, but it's new and he's still learning." There. I'd been partially truthful. Calling his Gift Dianic would immediately make it seem less powerful to Arden. It wasn't Elemental. But what she didn't know was that Ivan didn't really need any of the Gifts combined to create what he did. He just…in essence…was the Gift itself. Like a big, walking modem.

Or that's how I explained it to myself this week. Give it time. It'll change as his abilities changed, that I was sure of.

"Really?" Arden leaned in closer to Ivan who immediately sent me a text. It appeared in the air in front of me, red this time. All of it was red.

I'm accessing your Arcane thing. This way she can't see the messages with her magic.

I didn't nod or acknowledge. And I didn't know how to text back so I just smiled.

I can't talk to you like I did before because this house's surveillance isn't electronic. It's magical. I mean it's on a different electromagnetic field. "So, you guys going to tell me what the hell happened and why Kyle's not answering my calls?"

We brought Ivan up to speed, each of telling our part. As he listened, he touched his tablet as if working. I knew what he was doing since he and I had already discussed clandestine use of his magic before. The tablet was the focus he used to access the Internet. This way he could use the screen and still be tactile without projecting what he found into the air in front of him. So instead of building the virtual Cyber World around him, he was technically half-diving into the machine itself, putting half his consciousness into the Internet. To anyone else, especially Arden, it would look like he was just hacking on a tablet when it was so much more.

Did I understand it?

No.

Did I think it was brilliant?

Hell yes.

While Arden finished her part about coming to the rescue and sweeping me out of harm's way, Ivan continued to nod and move at a breakneck speed over the tablet's surface with his fingers. Grey settled herself on the couch, practically on top of me. I was surprised Arden didn't say something given there was a really big animal on her nice furniture. I kept a hand on Grey's back the whole time, feeling better the longer she and I were together.

The fact she was my mother in another form didn't negate the fact she'd proxied herself as my familiar. She still gave me her strength and her support. Mentally and physically. I loved the combination… but there were times I really just wanted her back as I remembered her. As a human. I just wanted a warm hug.

"I've…" Ivan said with his eyes glued to the screen. "I've tapped into the traffic cameras around Circe's home and within a hundred mile radius. Rewinding back to the event…" He stopped talking as his eyes widened.

What you guys did on some of these recordings should not be seen. I'm going to download them and then wipe them.

Now I was a bit nervous. I was always afraid Ivan was going to get caught.

"I see…" Ivan moved his hands over the tablet. Arden leaned over to look. "I see Miss Vervain's people picking you up, Sam. And if I move to another camera…"

I pushed Grey back and got up so I could stand behind the sofa he and Arden were sitting on and look over his shoulder. Bastien joined me.

Ivan had the screen broken up into six different views from six different surveillance cameras, most of them traffic cams. The cams' movements were fluid but jumpy. I watched as Bastien picked me up, he was naked cause I could see his full moon, and set me inside one of Arden's black vans. Another camera watched us drive away. And still another caught a brief glimpse to the side of Levi half carrying, half supporting Crwys to something off camera. I assumed they went to Crwys's Mustang.

"What's that?" Arden pointed to the view in the lower right corner.

Ivan moved his fingers over it to bring it to the front. It looked like a side view of the neighborhood and bunch of dark figures shoving two other hooded figures into the back of a van. "I think that's Kyle and Jack."

"Why didn't Jack just wolf out and tear them apart?" That boneheaded question came from me.

I say boneheaded because Arden looked at us and pulled back. "Jack's a Lycan? My nephew is sleeping with a Lycan?"

Bastien came to the rescue and put a hand on her shoulder. "It is safe, *chérie*. He is apogee and is ruled by the moon at this time. When Audrianna is in her full glory, he has no control of the shift, and will remain in what we call our war form. The upright beast. But between the Goddesses' glories, he can shift to full wolf."

Arden wasn't really keen on it though. "Look, that's mighty wolfie of you to accept their relationship, especially since your kind is all into testosterone and domination and Jack and Kyle are so far on the other end of that, but I'm not sure I can approve of this. When we get them back, you and I are going to have a sit down with them and lay down a few ground rules." She pointed at herself and Bastien.

He looked at me and half smiled. "*Je regrette*. I now see why you fight with this one."

"I got a license plate." Ivan moved off the pages of screens and into a DOT database I was pretty sure he shouldn't have access to. "The van is registered to Olivia Graham."

"You'd think she would have hidden that," Arden tapped the screen. "Can you track the van?"

"I can to a point," Ivan pulled up the screens again. "Combining all of the traffic sightings on the van until it moved away from cameras, it was heading this way."

"This way? Did you find any other houses in her financials with an address near here?" Arden asked.

"Yep. I'll bet that's where she took them and where she's holding Marilla." He tapped the screen again and within seconds he smiled. "This is interesting," he paused. "Sam, didn't Blackwood say he didn't have any dealings with Olivia Graham?"

"Yeah. Why?"

"Because he's half-owner of a company that owns a house that backs up to this property. Look," Ivan turned the tablet for us to see better. "Right there under primary—look at the secondary owner."

Olivia Graham. This did not bode well. Not at all. I wrapped my arms around my chest. "I don't understand. He seemed genuinely disgusted with Olivia Graham's actions."

Arden snorted. "Edmund Blackwood isn't genuine about anything, Samantha. Remember that. I knew he owned the property next to mine, but I didn't know he had a house on it. I've sent dozens of neophytes out there to snoop just because I like to see who's near my borders," she didn't look so confident anymore. "Now I'm pissed off thinking that crazy bitch could be so close to my own power base."

"Maybe we should go take a look ourselves?" I asked.

Arden gestured to the tablet with her hand. "You're not going to find that house even if you found the address. Not if my own people never saw it. Magicians are notorious for camouflage and deceit. You could walk or take a boat in the bayou for days and go right past it." She shook her head.

Bastien moved to the fireplace and stoked the flames. "Then where do we go from here? I can't hear Jack, none of the pack can touch him. It's like it was when Marilla and André disappeared."

"If we can't get to her, then we need her to come to us," I said and crossed my arms over my chest. I started pacing behind the sofa, only I wasn't really aware I was doing it. "If she comes to us then she'll leave the house. All we need is something that will expose the house. Something that'll break through a Magician's barriers. And we need something that will nullify her magic."

"That's a lot of needs," Ivan looked up from the tablet. "I can do a search online."

"I have an idea," Arden said.

I found myself staring at Bastien.

"What do you have in mind?" Bastien asked, oblivious to the fact I was shivering and staring at him.

"We use our magic rules against theirs."

None of us figured it out at first. I forced my attention away from Bastien and sat back down on the couch with Grey. Having her wet nose in my ear and against my neck helped clear my head. Okay, pull it together, Sam. Use the two magic rules against one another. So what made their rules different than ours? Well it was going back to basics again. Witches blessed and invited the Elements in. Ceremonial Magicians cast Circles to keep…things…*out*. "Oh!" I looked at Arden. "I get it. But how are we going to do that? If you haven't detected a house and they're using deceit and subterfuge, that means there's a self-sustaining spell surrounding the place. Like a barrier."

"That's what we have to come up with. I'll call my coven together to help. Bastien, we're going to need your pack as well. Once we get into that house, I want to look for some items Circe allegedly stole from Blackwood."

"Yeah, he mentioned stolen stuff." Arden rarely did anything that didn't benefit her. She took full credit for those missing children. Getting a nephew back from a crazy person would be enough of a reward for anyone else, but not Arden. If she actually returned stolen items to their rightful owners, i.e. Blackwood, or confiscated Magician tools for the Witches, then it all looked good for her. If she just happened to save her nephew and rescue two wolves for the Aces, great for her!

It bothered me she would use this for her own gain, but I wanted Kyle and Jack out of there more, and I really wanted that wolf girl back with her pack so I could stop wanting to rip Bastien's clothes off.

I'd do anything for Kyle. And the thought of that bitch using one of her potions on him burned my chest.

Bastien clapped his hands together. "My pack will find the house if it is truly there."

Ah. Good idea. Send the pack out to sniff around for it. They could lock onto the specific Arcane smell.

So...why was I feeling like I'd made a really big mistake by leaving this up to Arden?

-She's going to betray you.-

"Yeah," I said under my breath as Bastien and Arden worked out the pack participation details. "I just don't know how."

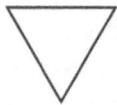

EIGHTEEN

I half listened to their plan as we sat in Arden's dining room. Her chef had prepared a filling meal. Three trays of club sandwiches. Turkey, ham and roast beef. Five different kinds of homemade chips. Potato salad and a broccoli stem slaw. I nibbled here and there but didn't have much of an appetite. And that was bad. Normally, if I knew I was going to be using a bunch of magic I'd eat a big meal.

Ivan sat at the far end of the table with a plate of food and his tablet. He was still searching as he ate, keeping up appearances of someone playing a game. Arden had brought out maps of the bayou, especially around her home. If the van carrying Kyle and Jack had been heading in that direction, there were over fifty ways they could have gone. Bastien called in his Beta, a charming little Cajun girl named Molly. She was small, but I sensed power around her and knew she was probably a kick-ass wolf. She was perigee, same as Bastien.

Why couldn't he take *her* as a mate?

A text box appeared across the top of my roast beef club. **I followed the Mustang and I have an address. But you're not going to believe where it is.**

I didn't look up and waited for his revelation.

When he typed out the address I gasped. No. I didn't believe it. This was a block away from Ina's home in the Garden District.

I checked the address with Crwys's financials and he's not even closely affiliated with the house. It's not Levi's either. It belongs to some company called Mephistopheles, Inc.

Didn't ring a bell for me but if that's where Levi took Crwys, then that's where I was going. And I could stop by my place and pick up my phone charger.

"Sam, you all right, *shugah*?"

I looked up at Arden and then pushed my chair out. "Yeah I'm fine. I just need to get over to my shop."

"Why? It's locked up secure and all. Your boy down there said so."

"I need some things from my apartment," I looked at Ivan. "Did you want to come with me?"

"I think he should stay here with us," Arden put her hands on the table. "His skills with a computer could come in useful, and if you don't make it back before the pack finds Circe's base, then I'll have a way to get in touch with you."

I wanted to argue with her. I wanted Ivan with me because, right now, I had bells and whistles going off around her. She was up to something, and I was afraid that something involved Brendi and the price for information about the Changeling children. I didn't have proof. I just had that nagging feeling I always got when something was going to go wrong.

Goddess I hated that feeling.

I opened my mouth to suggest Ivan come with me, but his next text stopped me. **Go find Crwys. I can spy on Arden and Bastien. Keep you updated.**

With a swift hug to Ivan, who gave me his keys, Grey and I headed outside to his truck and got the hell out of Gypsy Gardens. The drive back into town was pleasant enough. Not a lot of tourist traffic in the middle of the day.

The house matching the address was a monster. Don't get me wrong, Ina's house looked like the house out of *Candle Magic*, but it still wasn't as big as this one. This antebellum was the mother of all antebellum houses. Two story, with the infamous black wrought iron around its verandas, as well as the property itself. The place had a double oak door with stained glass on either side. That much I could see from the road as I parked the truck right in front. "Park fu" is my copilot.

That's a nice house.

"Uh huh. Looks like it could fit three families." I got out of the truck and came around the side to let Grey out. The gate was locked but there was a buzzer. I rang it.

Levi's voice came through the speaker. "No deliveries today."

I pressed the button and held it. "Levi, it's Sam. I need to see Crwys."

I heard some swearing on the other side. "No Sam. Sorry. He's not—"

Then I heard Crwys's voice in the background. I waited, Grey and I looked at each other.

The gate buzzed and the speaker turned off.

I guess that means we can come in.

"Yeah." I hurried up the concrete walk, noting the gigantic oak in the front yard and the swing hanging from it. Solar powered lights were spaced out evenly along the walk's edges amid a colorful array of pansies. "This is so not Crwys's house."

Just as we got to the door, it opened. I stopped when I saw Crwys, wearing only a pair of soft, worn jeans and a whole lot of bruises. They littered this chest, arms and stomach. His hair was mussed and his eyes looked bruised. What caught me more off guard were the emotions rolling over me like waves along a shore. Relief, happiness, frustration, disappointment, desire and above all—possession.

This man was mine.

I knew it in that instant. I didn't know how. Might have been the way his eyes moved up and down my body and his mouth hung open.

"Crwys…" I ventured. He looked like he'd frozen in place.

What I didn't expect him to do was rush forward and grab me. Both of his arms came around my own in a breath-taking embrace. He buried his face in my neck and I felt him kissing me. He released me, grabbed my face and gave me the longest, deepest and most sensual kiss he'd ever given me.

I had to blink a few times to realign myself when he stopped. His amber red eyes searched my face. "You're alive."

"So…so are you."

"Come in. Grey. Please, both of you come in," he stepped back and waved us in.

When the door closed I turned to him and he kissed me again. "Crwys—"

"No. Not here. Come in here. Levi and I need to be brought up to speed."

When I turned, I got the enormity of the house thrown in my face again. Sweet Lord and Lady! The foyer was the size of my entire apartment! The floor was white and beige marble, with a huge six-foot floral arrangement in the center beneath a three-tiered chandelier. A single staircase moved upstairs to the left just past the flowers and behind that was a living room, complete with fireplace and flat screen

TV. I could see a row of closed doors to either side of it and I wondered if those doors opened up to a pool.

The room he guided us to looked like a smaller version of the room behind the stairs. The room's theme was green and gold, with a light beige carpet that sucked my low-heeled boots right down.

The walls were painted a forest green and the curtains were gold and pulled tight. A fireplace to the left heated the place and the two couches looked as if Levi and Crwys had been sleeping on them. White sheets half sagged off the sides of one and a mount of pillows still had the indentation of an occupant.

Levi lounged on the other couch, a stack of books in front of him on the coffee table. I bent over to look and noticed several big names in mystery. "Wow Levi, I never pegged you for a mystery fan."

"I am. And just so you know, I am not happy about you and the wolf being in here. This house is supposed to be off the grid, so to speak."

I assumed he meant the magical grid. "This is a safe house, isn't it? For Revenants?"

Now Levi sat up and stared at me. "How did you know that?"

"What else could it be? This isn't Crwys's place."

Crwys came up behind me and guided me to the couch with the sheets draped over it. He sat at one end and I sat at the other. Grey insinuated herself on the couch between us. "You look...incredible."

"You look like shit. Crwys...what happened?"

"He thought you were dead," Levi said as he tossed a book on the pile. "You looked dead. So when he stupidly tried to get in that beast's way, he got mauled."

I took a closer look at Crwys, at the bruises and the marks and remembered the thing sinking its teeth into him. "It bit you."

"Yeah, two places," Crwys touched his shoulder. "But it's almost healed now."

"Because you drank Levi's blood, right? That's why you two have been holed up in here?"

I sure hoped the two of them never played poker because they could not keep the guilty looks off their faces. When they exchanged glances I waved at them. "Look, all I need to know is are you Levi's Ghoul? Is that why my *dex* can't figure out what you are?"

Levi threw his head back with a deep, heart-filled laugh. Crwys threw a pillow at Levi. Grey snorted and kicked her back leg at Crwys.

"Ow," he said before he rubbed her back. "Your mom's not happy I left you alone."

"That was my fault, Grey," Levi sat forward. "I realized how bad Crwys was hurt so I got him out of there."

"But not to a hospital," I narrowed my eyes. "If he's not your Ghoul then why not a hospital?"

"That would bring questions we really don't want to deal with," Crwys reached out and put his hand on my shoulder, over Grey's back. "I've never said I was human."

"No you haven't, but you've also never told me what you are."

"And it's not time. So…" he squeezed my shoulder. "Tell us what's happened."

"First, *you* two need to tell *me* what happened. Like why were you in that house in the front room with Bastien and Circe?"

The two of them looked at one another. "We don't know," Levi said. "We saw Jack outside and then went up the steps to knock on the door and then…" he said and shrugged. "We were sitting in the room with Bastien and I could hear all kinds of shit happening outside."

"Yeah," Crwys said. "I was woozy. Real dizzy and I stumbled to the window. I could see this big ass monster wolf-man tossing you around like a boss so I ran outside and got in its way." He squeezed my shoulder again. "I really, really thought you were dead."

"No. And I've been worried about you."

"Okay," Levi rubbed his hands together. "Your turn. Fill us in."

So I did. I started from where Kyle and I arrived, what we did, what Circe said and ended with me waking up at Arden's mansion. When I told them about her suggestion there could be things in there that would destroy Circe, Crwys shrugged. "I don't know. Magicians are still a new thing for me."

"New thing? Seriously?" I looked at him.

"Witches have been around since the beginning. Gaia and Diana are your patrons. But Magicians don't really follow any doctrine that I know of. They're pretty much all for themselves. I would assume your weaknesses are theirs."

"No." I rubbed at his hand on my shoulder. His skin was warmer than ever. If he were human, I'd say he had a fever. But this was normal for him. And I knew my temperature was still up. "A weakness would be exhaustion. But even that's different for me than it is for Kyle. I don't know how Magicians's work magic."

Ritual. Grey pressed her nose into my side. *They use a combination of Hedge Magic with Elemental, though they've warped it over the years.*

"How is theirs different?" Crwys asked Grey. Apparently he'd been able to hear Grey since the day they met.

Rudimentary usage. For instance, before Sam was warlocked, her Elementals manifested at her call and made the magic for her, but they also used her thoughts and will, as well as her essence for the three laws.

Crwys frowned.

"The different levels things affect us. Mental, physical and spiritual. My Elementals are a part of me so they work with me," I said.

As for Kyle and his Hedge Witchery. He works with the Elements, the colors, the sounds of words in a spell…the cadence and the herbs.

"I still don't get it."

"We work *with*, become a part *of* and give ourselves *to*. But a Ceremonial commands, breaks and transforms all with their will. There's no cooperation on any level except the basic need or want for something," I sat forward. "What Arden's suggesting we do is bring the things they're afraid of inside. We find Circe's barriers, cut a new Circle along the edge and invite in the Elementals." I grinned. "It'd be like trapping them in a cage with their worst nightmares."

Levi chuckled. "I like this idea."

"So do I. That way they'll be so busy freaking out that we can go in and grab Kyle, Marilla and Jack. Will they stop Circe?"

"I don't know. We'll have to play it by ear."

"Don't trust Arden," Levi said as stood and stretched. "Just remember that. Don't. Trust. Vervain. This is a good plan. What do you need to do?"

"I need to get back there. Make sure they do what they say they're going to do and save Kyle and Jack."

Crwys put his hand on mine. "And look for that Codex."

"Yeah."

Levi smirked. "I'm gonna take a shower. You go save the world," he pointed to Crwys. "And you are staying put."

"Like shit I am. I'm not letting Sam put her life in danger again."

This time I scooted Grey off the couch and moved closer to him. "Yes you are. You're going to stay here and heal."

He pulled me close. "How, exactly, are you going to make me?"

And once Levi left the room with Grey behind him, I showed him exactly how I was going to make him.

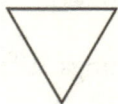

NINETEEN

I shoved the charger into the phone once Grey and I were upstairs in my apartment. I pulled out my usual uniform of jeans, shirt and one of my older jackets. Not leather, but denim. I had to take a shower, just because I needed to not smell like sex when I met up with Bastien.

Do you have any clothes like that in your closet?

I looked over at Grey where she'd sprawled on my bed. "I have some things. You know…stuff I bought during my Stevie Nicks phase, which is a phase I tend to go in and out of. I've also got this killer club dress in here, white, but there's nowhere in New Orleans to wear it. Why?"

Because Crwys liked you in that skirt. And you look pretty in it.

I stared at the wolf. "I do?"

Honey, I know this isn't the time for this conversation, but we really need to have a talk about your wardrobe. And don't give me that look. At least you can still wear clothes.

I couldn't help but smile as I jumped on the bed beside her and gave her a big hug. "I love having you with me."

I wouldn't want to be anywhere else. Now, get cleaned up so we can bring the boys home.

The water in my apartment runs either really hot or really cold. There is no middle ground, and there's no rhyme or reason as to which temperature is chosen for any particular shower. Or when the shower is taken. It never failed that when Crwys took a shower he always got the extreme cold. I swear I thought I saw steam coming out of the bathroom when that happened.

What I normally did to combat this inconvenience was to summon my Undine to balance the temperature. She was always happy to do it as long as I stopped up the sink and filled it with water so she could hang out while I showered. She would splash and sing, most likely a siren's song, which didn't affect me. But since the warlocking that wasn't possible. I'd been taking my showers in silence and alone.

But I was still in the habit of filling the sink. When I realized what I'd done, I just left it there.

My phone pinged in the other room with a text message. I debated going back in to see, but if it was Ivan telling me they found the house, he could send me one of his floaty glowing text boxes.

When I got in the shower this time, the water was scalding hot. I figured if I left the window open it would balance the heat. It wasn't going to stop my skin from turning red, but I could soothe it afterward with cooling lotion. Stepping in, I was shivering at the cold and thought of ritual baths and how it might be a good idea if I brought the three of us back into the Old Ways a little at time. Having the full moon ritual had been a good idea. It wasn't my fault a pack of Lycans showed up and sort of changed everything.

It was during that scalding shower, with me going from shivering to sticking my head out of the shower to escape the water that I thought I heard a commotion nearby. At first, I assumed it was something outside. I lived on Bourbon Street, after all. And the noise to drunk ratio was pretty high. I took another few minutes to rinse off as the water started evening out to something very nice, much like my Undine would keep it.

When I shut the water off, I heard Grey barking, snarling and banging on the bathroom door. But she wasn't talking to me.

"Mom?" I said aloud, wondering if she could hear me.

That's when my ears popped in a very familiar way. The only time my ears popped like that was when a cap had been placed. But only Clerics did caps. Oh crap—was the Hive here? Downstairs? Was that why Grey was trying to get my attention?

I grabbed the towel hanging over the curtain rod and wrapped myself in it. When I pulled the curtain away, I found myself face to face with the barrel of a gun with a silencer. Holding that gun was the robed and angry looking Fred. And I was holding nothing but a towel.

"Go on, Samantha. Step out of the shower."

I'd been in a lot of sticky situations, but never anything like this. I was unprepared and silently panicking. Grey continued to run at the door, snarling and barking and I was still curious as to why she wasn't talking to me. Was it the cap? No…it couldn't be that. But then…how would I know since I'd only had one visit from the Hive since learning Grey was my mom and could talk to me?

Pulling the towel tight around me, I stepped down and moved into the corner at the foot of the tub. It wasn't a very large bathroom. Just enough space for a tub, sink and toilet. The tile was like ice under my feet and I was dripping all over it. "Hi Fred."

"Shut the hell up." Fred's tone was so full of hatred it hurt to hear. This guy hated me.

"What are you doing here?" There. I think I sounded pretty good, considering I was a blithering idiot on the inside.

He held that gun steady as he pointed it at my head. "I want to know why you're not going crazy. I want to know why you're not falling apart like my dad did. His warlocking destroyed him, it tore him apart from the inside out until he cut his own throat at the dinner table one night."

Was he serious? Oh damn. I had no idea. And I assumed this was something Fred had seen which, of course, had emotionally scarred him. How in the hell had Cromwell approved this man to be a freak'n Cleric with this kind of emotional trauma?

He pushed the gun at me and I backed up. The wall stopped me and I knocked over a few hair products. "Answer me!"

"I don't know!" I used one hand to hold up the towel and held the other up in defense. "Maybe Cromwell did something different?"

"It's all the same. And it's not right. You were supposed to suffer the same way!"

I felt warmth grow in my chest and I knew this was not going to end well if I didn't calm Fred down. "I didn't do anything to your dad, Fred. That was my mom. That was another time."

"Your mom is dead, so that leaves you. You're the only one I have left to punish."

"Why—why do you have to punish me? It's not going to bring your dad back, and it's sure as hell not going to make you feel better."

"See? You don't get it, do you? You don't know me. You don't know anything about me. I have to punish you because she says that's the only way."

She? I caught that. But it was getting hard to hear him over Grey's insistent slamming against the door. She was really freaking out and I could tell it was wearing on Fred as well. *Mom! Stop! He's crazy!*

But there was no answer other than the angry wolf noises on the other side of the bathroom door.

"Shut that damn mutt up!" Yeah, Fred was losing it.

"Grey! Be quiet!" I hoped she would hear me and stop when I glanced past him to the door that vibrated every time she threw herself against it. That's when I saw something moving at the sink.

Undines are interesting things. Elementals in general are. Mostly because they don't really have form, other than what we give them. Sort of like the Destructor in *Ghostbusters*. That particular character let someone else choose what form to take. Elementals were the same. Once they bonded with their Witch, the two agreed on a shape that would always be recognizable. Most of them came in the usual commercial packages because as a group we'd all watched the same movies and read the same books.

My Undine was a mermaid. But not just any sort. She was blue, green and mother of pearl and she looked like me in the face. That was her idea. A little joke, I'm sure. But her tail was that of a betta fish, with beautiful hues of blues and greens. It undulated beautifully behind her as she moved through air and water.

I would know her anywhere.

So what I didn't understand was why or how she was sitting on the edge of my sink with her tail in the water I'd left there, watching us. Miss Water of the Clerics had my Undine. That's what Cromwell had done when he'd sealed them away from me. The seal apparently prevented me from immediately knowing she was there. I wasn't in control of her.

Fred turned to see what I was staring at but it was obvious he didn't see her. "What? You look freaked out."

"Nothing. I mean, I'm naked in my bathroom and you're holding a gun on me. I *am* little freaked out."

That made him smile. "Good. I want you to be freaked out, and you'll be more freaked out when you find out what's in store for you."

"In store for me?"

"Oh, we're not done with you yet."

Uh…what? We? "Fred, who's we?"

He moved the gun again and pressed the silencer to my forehead, ignoring my question. "And since you're not this Elemental Witch anymore and just a plain old Cowen, I can make you dance like a puppet," he smiled at me. "Drop the towel."

Grey charged at the door again and barked.

"No."

"No? You think I'm kidding here?"

You know…I was getting irritated now. One of the things we're taught from an early age is not to use our power against the Cowens. We were born to protect this world, not fuck it up. One of my biggest pet peeves was dickheads like this guy thinking just because they were born with the right kind of blood in their veins they had the right to use it for their personal gain. I straightened my shoulders as I narrowed my eyes.

-*He's going to shoot us.*-

Us?

My phone rang.

He shoved the gun against my head this time and it hurt. "Drop the damn towel!"

I glared at him. "No." Don't get me wrong. I was scared as hell and shaking like a vibrator with new batteries.

Grey charged the door again.

Fred swore. "Shut that dog up!"

-*We should get rid of him. He's never going to leave us alone.*-

"God damn it!" Fred swung the gun around to point it at the door. He was going to shoot through the wood at Grey.

-*All you have to do is put it all together.*-

The voice was soothing against the turmoil in my head. The next few minutes were like a John Woo slow motion capture for me as I lunged at him. My intent was to grab the gun from him so he wouldn't shoot Grey. Beyond that—I hadn't given it much thought. But the voice in my head had.

I saw my hand shoot out as I lunged at Fred. My chest burned as if someone pressed a soldering iron into it and I screamed out as I wrapped my hand around his hand holding the gun. Many things went through my mind at that moment. One of them was wishing this son of a bitch would just disappear. The thought was tinged with the same red hue as my wish to survive last night had been, when that thing had lunged at me from across the street and then disappeared.

I smelled something burning, something acrid, something electrical as I stumbled forward and slammed into the door. The door opened outward as it gave with my weight and I did an excellent spill on the floor. Grey was immediately in my face licking me and then dashing into the bathroom.

But Fred wasn't there.

And I was holding the gun.

"Oh no…" I said aloud and I immediately looked at the sink,

just visible past the door where it stuck out from the white tile. My Undine was there, watching me, before she vanished in a bubble pop.

—Believe you can't hear me! Come on, Sam. Listen to me! Where is that bastard? Where did he go? And was that an Undine I just saw—

"Mom!" I dropped the gun and put my hands to my ears. My towel was little more than a limp bundle by that time but I didn't care. It was just us women now, because Fred was nowhere to be seen.

Oh thank the Lord and Lady! I've been screaming at you ever since you got in there. I heard that bastard on the fire escape. Where is he? She turned around in the bathroom and looked at me. Then she looked at the gun on the hall's hardwood floor and went to sniff it. *This is his. Did he jump out the window?*

"No…no…" I put my hands to my face and then put them over my chest. The spot where the mark was felt hot and when I looked down, the scar was more pronounced. It was a big disk of puckering, pinkish skin.

Sam?

I looked at Grey and felt my eyes ache as emotion overwhelmed me. I'd come a hair's breath away from a plethora of things. Of possibly being raped, of being beaten, of being murdered…and my Undine had seen me destroy another human being with Arcane. The smell permeated the bathroom. It clung to my skin. It lived in my hair. It was awful.

Grey moved in beside me and crouched down, inching her snout under my hands to my face. *Sam-Sam? What is it?*

I wiped at my face as the emotion came and went in waves. I was good one minute and then bad the next. And then good again and stayed that way for a few minutes. "I…Mom I think I just destroyed that man."

You did?

"Yeah…the way I destroyed the thing that attacked me outside Circe's. Fred was there one minute and then gone the next. Mom…my Undine saw!"

So that was your Undine. How was she here?

"Mom…don't you get it? She saw what I did. She'll report it to Miss Water of the Clerics and then Cromwell will know I'm using Arcane…I'm being consumed by Arcane and they'll make a vote to kill me."

Mom did a good wolf impression of a snort. *They'll have to get through me.*

My phone rang again. Grey pushed herself up and retrieved it from the desk, pulling the charger out of the wall and dragging it along with the phone to me. I smiled at her and wiped her saliva off of it. It was Ivan. "Hey, I figured you'd send a text message."

"I tried but you weren't receiving. It was like you were offline."

Huh. I'd been so offline even my mom couldn't talk to me. "I was taking a shower. What's up?" I thought I sounded pretty good considering what had just happened. But then, what did that say about me? I had just killed someone. That made two people. The bodies were stacking up.

"The Aces found the house. It's a mansion about ten miles inside the marker between Arden's property and Mr. Blackwood's. Arden swears she's been all over that property and never saw it. She's got her coven in the area coordinating getting the Circle cut. You coming?"

"I'll be there."

"Oh, bring the water out of your sink."

I froze. "Wh-what?"

"Bring the water out of your sink."

"Where did you get that?"

"I don't know. It was on a piece of paper a member of the coven gave me. I assume it's a request from Arden. See you in a bit."

I disconnected before he could and let the phone drop.

By taking the water in my sink, I would be giving my Undine access to wherever I went because she'd touched it. Someone already *knew* my Undine had been in my sink. Ivan assumed it was a message from Arden.

Was it possible…however remotely…that she was working with the Clerics? Was Arden the mysterious *she* Fred mentioned? Was… and this sounded even more ridiculous…was Arden working with Cromwell to get rid of me?

Or worse, make me weak and useless and easier to give to the Obsidian Queen?

Either way, I needed to get going. I also needed to get rid of the gun. For now, I wrapped it in a clean towel and shoved it into the bag with the other ritual supplies.

If my wild imagination had any part of it based in reality, then I was in a lot of danger and so were those around me. It was time to go on the offensive, so I wouldn't be caught on the defensive.

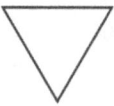

TWENTY

Trying to set aside panic at what I'd just done to another human being, I grabbed a mason jar and filled it with water from my sink. The rest I let spiral down the drain. My hands shook, my body shook, and not all of it was from my emotional terror at that moment. The wolf fever had ramped its take over up a few notches. I was running out of time, and I had no idea how I was going to explain Fred's disappearance.

All my mind wanted to focus on was Arwen's death at my hands using Arcane, the catalyst that set all of this off, the destruction of my dad's house and their bodies, and now Fred. There was no way I could keep doing this and not get caught. And if Cromwell caught wind of what was really going on, not get killed. I had to think of some logical explanation for Fred's disappearance. Some plausible excuse that would make everyone happy. I didn't know if he had any family remaining that would miss him, though I somehow doubted it. But if he did, family was usually the one thing that didn't stop until it got answers. I was still surprised Arwen's family hadn't shown up asking where their daughter was.

Still shaking, still freaked out, I dressed with shaking hands but managed to get everything in place.

I dumped a bunch of stuff into my bag, including the mason jar, my own white handled knife and then agonized over whether to keep the gun in my bag for about five minutes. Truth was I'd rather have it with me than leave it there. That's when I realized I didn't have my own guns. Where were my guns? The last place I remembered using them was outside Circe's house. And I'd thrown them into the back of my Jeep.

I assumed my Jeep was still parked across the street from Circe's.

I didn't have time to retrieve it. According to Ivan's directions, Circe's base of power was in the opposite direction. The GPS map told me I was going to be on the road for at least forty minutes. Great. I had forty minutes to relive what just happened and try not to self-condemn my actions.

No. You'll have me with you.

I looked at Grey as she stood by the door. "No. I can't risk you, mom. I—I don't think I could keep going if you weren't here."

I'm not going anywhere. And I can take care of myself. I'm not entirely helpless.

I had sort of suspected the part about her not being helpless. I just didn't know in what way. I didn't know if Faerie paladins had special powers. Other than the fact they were previously human. I didn't know if they were all human, but mom had let me know that all of the ones she'd met and befriended had been. The whole idea of stealing humans out of this world, transforming them and then taking them back to *Alfheim* pissed me off. I thought the Faerie Queens should spend time as wolves. See what it's like.

"Okay. So," I put my bag over my shoulder and gestured for her to precede me down the steps. "Let's get going."

I locked the shop up again and agonized over where to put my things in Ivan's truck. He didn't have a locker I could use in the back, and I was afraid a lot of bouncing and tossing around would destroy the mason jar. I carefully placed everything in the floorboard of the passenger side as Grey jumped in and immediately plopped down.

I thought Ivan had a Mini-Cooper.

"He does. And he has a truck. And no, I don't know where his Mini-Cooper is."

I like that car.

Since my cell phone was now fully charged, I diverted Ivan from sending me text updates—since we're not supposed to text and drive—to talking to me over the speaker on my phone. It was sometime after midnight. I was out late again, starting to really feel the fever of the Lycan change, and running on leftover Chinese food and club sandwiches. Oh and with little to no sleep, other than what I'd had at Arden's earlier in the day.

The thing in or on my chest, I couldn't tell which anymore, felt heavy and hot. It protruded now, something I noticed after my run in with Fred.

Fred.

Stop it. Grey's voice had a bit of a growl to it in my head. *He was going to do unspeakable things to you. You defended yourself.*

"Mom, I don't know that."

She paused. *I do.*

I glanced over at her when we reached a light. "You heard his thoughts?"

Loud and clear. He planned on raping you and dismantling you so no one would ever find your body.

The car behind me honked their horn. I'd been staring at Grey, not wanting to believe what she just said. The thought that someone hated me *that* much just wouldn't compute for me. I moved the truck forward and processed this new information. It didn't really make me feel better about what I'd done, but it helped me slot what happened into some kind of place that could make sense to me. The same place I'd slotted what I did to Kennett. It was all done in defense, to right a wrong or defend my life.

"Heard whose thoughts?" Ivan's voice came over the phone's tiny speaker.

"Nobody's," I answered. "Any news?"

"They've found the seam of Circe's protection barrier. Arden's putting her people out around the barrier, spacing them at the four quarters. She wants to know if you'd be willing to stand in for Water."

Grey and I exchanged glances.

I'm not sure that's a good idea.

"Me either." And I was pretty sure my mom hesitated for the same reason I did. Arcane. To mix my magic into a sacred Circle with three other participants…I didn't know if that was enough to corrupt their magic as well. "Ivan, I'm still a good half an hour away. And tell her my fever's up, so I don't think it's a good idea."

"Roger."

I really was half an hour away, and as I finished the drive, taking the truck off road and down a few really, really dark service roads, Ivan kept me updated. Arden started the initial cut at the north, and because the distance was so great, she wouldn't be able to hold the power long enough to move the blade the entire circumference. Therefore, when she started the cut going deosil, clockwise, she anchored the first quarter at the east. The Witch at the east would then connect to the cut and move to the south and anchor the now half Circle there. The Witch at the south would follow to the west, and then the west back to the north where the Circle would be connected. The whole endeavor had to be done at the same speed with no stops or gaps to keep the momentum going. A Witch's Circle wasn't stagnate; it moved in a spiral, in a constant deosil direction.

I felt the hum and vibration in my bones as I neared the entrance to a long dirt road. And with the Arcane I could actually see the magnificent sphere Arden and her coven had created. It reached far above the trees and fathoms below the ground. A ginormous egg of the God Mother's power. The hairs on my arms stood on end as I stopped the truck and got out. Grey followed me and we stood just outside of its whirling iridescence.

"It's a good thing I didn't put my magic into that."

Yeah. I didn't realize Arden had become so…powerful.

"That's not just her. It's the power of her coven combined."

Still…be careful around her. This is the swamp and Water is her Elemental Gift.

"You sound a little worried. Do you sense Faeries?"

No. But I got that feeling. Call it a Witch's intuition.

Yeah, I knew what she meant. So did I.

A sharp pain sliced through my head, just behind my eyes and the door I'd shut on the pack link cracked.

<Bonjour, ma petite. I am happy you're here,> came Bastien's voice in my mind.

Dammit. I thought I'd finally shoved him out. And I hated the way my body reacted the second that link was re-established. I could smell him. Feel his heat against me. And in the back of my mind, he was all I wanted.

<Where is everyone? I'm at the end of the road.> I sent the thought back, not really sure if he could hear it.

Guess what! He did! *<Come in further. We are a quarter of a mile inside.>*

Grey heard him too. I pulled stuff from the truck, making sure the mason jar was intact, and we started the hike in the dark. Well, it wasn't really dark for us with magical sight. The big spinning sphere cast everything in a silver glow.

I sensed everyone before I arrived. The group had staked out a clearing and set up an altar on a card table. This was north, the start and end of the Circle now closing off the base inside of it. Arden and her group were dressed in fashionable black, some in skirts, others in tights and a few in black jeans. The quarter callers were all dressed in robes and standing in their own circle behind the altar, keeping their concentration on the Circle.

"Glad you could make it," Arden said as she approached. She had an odd look on her face. Not really happy, but not sad. More like, determined. "We're about to invite the Elementals. Want to Call?"

"No," I shook my head. "You're doing a great job. What's the plan?"

"Once we Call, the Elementals will have whatever reign they want."

"What about the barrier the Magicians set up?"

She laughed. It wasn't a particularly nice laugh. "It's in reverse polarity. Can you feel it?"

Reverse polarity meant the Magicians had created it going widdershins, counterclockwise. I listened, but I didn't hear anything but the hum of Arden's Circle. "No. I don't."

"Because we tore it down!" One of the other girls yelled out as she came toward us. I recognized Dayle, one of the participants that helped get the Changeling children back. She and I embraced and her ample breasts against my chest pushed the Arcane scar into my rib cage. I hissed when it pressed into my ribs.

"Oh, I'm sorry!" Dayle stood back. "Are you okay?"

"She was thrown around by a monster," Arden spoke up. "She's still a bundle of bruises."

Arden was only half right. My bruises were healing up fast. I wasn't sure if that was due to the Arcane influence or because of Bastien's wolf venom running through my veins. The thought of him brought on its own heat as I sensed him nearing me. He stepped out of the darkness wearing little more than a pair of jeans. Barefoot. And looking magnificent. Every hormone in my body lit up like a Lite-Brite toy as he stood in front of me. I had to fight not to cling to him, and it was a really hard fight.

"You've been with *diable*."

Everyone looked at me. I straightened my shoulders. "Yes, I have."

Arden stood beside a very still Bastien. "Oh? Is the detective okay?"

"Yes he is. He's healing up nicely. But he's still weak so he won't be here."

Bastien growled. "Good." With a scowl he turned and headed back into the darkness.

He is angry you slept with Crwys.

"Well screw him," I muttered under my breath. "I'm not his."

To him, and by his rules, you are. You're still marked and you haven't had the antidote.

"He'd better give me that antidote once we get Marilla back. Does he sense her inside?"

No. But he and his pack are around the perimeter, all in wolf form. Waiting.

Ah. That explained the way Bastien was dressed. It had to be easier to become a wolf with less clothing on.

I hadn't realized Arden was watching me. I looked at her and raised my brow. "What?"

"You don't know the antidote."

"Do you?"

"Yes."

"So what is it?"

North Called the Elements in. Arden and I both reacted as we watched a plethora of Earth Elementals appear inside the sphere. They came in a variety of shapes, from Gnomes to Trolls to Rock Creatures and I thought I saw a character from a Nintendo game. These were the shapes taken by the Witches present. They headed deeper inside the sphere, intent on causing a little mischief.

East Called the Elementals. We didn't see them from where we stood in the north, but I knew they were there. I set my bag down on the ground beside a rock and noticed the mason jar had a slight sheen to it. I squatted down and pulled it from the bag as the south was called. Turning it around, I peered inside and found a small version of my face peering back at me. I gasped as my voice was lost in the calling of the west. My little Undine pointed to the lid and motioned for me to unscrew it.

I did as she asked and she vanished. Had she gone inside? How was it my Undine was here and not with Miss Water? Had something happened to the Cleric? Or had the Undine escaped?

Finally, the Calling was ended at the north. I could feel power radiating from the sphere as I stood and closed my eyes. I could also feel the pack through the now cracked door. I heard the cacophony that was their shared mind and followed along with the voice of Bastien as they waited until the right moment. That moment happened the instant the first fleeing Magician came running from the house and crossed the barrier.

One of the pack grabbed the Magician in its jaws, shook him and then tossed him to the side.

<Bastien! They can't kill them! That's mass murder!>

The pack grumbled at me but it was Bastien who answered. *<We're biting them to find their minds. If they survive, they will be pack!>*

I shook my head as I pushed the link aside and ran up to Arden. I grabbed her shoulder and spun her around. "They're attacking the Magicians!"

She pushed my hand off of her. "Yes. I know. That's how they can get into their minds to see who knows where our people are."

"But…that's going to turn some of them into Lycans!"

Arden's reaction freaked me out. She smiled. "That was my agreement with Bastien. They're just Magicians, Samantha. Once we get what we came for, he can have them all."

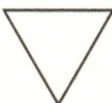

TWENTY ONE

We marched on Circe's power base as a unit. Arden's coven, Bastien's pack and my little group of myself, Ivan and Grey. Ivan had been inside of Arden's Mercedes, parked a little further back than where I left his truck. He told me as we walked through the woods he needed to be away from the use of magic to make his access to satellites via the tablet work. Made sense to me, even though I knew the electromagnetic fields of electronic devices weren't disrupted by magic when Ivan was around. It was all part of his Gift.

I was still reeling from Arden's revelation. She and Bastien had decided this without me. Possibly while I was with Crwys, or even while the Cleric was in my bathroom. And of course that thought led me right back to Fred and fretting about what I was going to do. I was also wigged out because of how much more upset I was about this than what I did to my dad's house. But if I thought about it, my dad was already dead when I got there, having been killed by Kennett. This... this was active.

But you did the same thing to the monster that attacked you at Circe's.

I glared down at Grey. "That's different."

I don't think so.

"What's different?" Ivan said as he kept up with us. "What are you two talking about?"

"Eh, nothing." I ducked under a branch, amazed at how easy it was for me to see in the darkness. The moon wasn't full anymore and tonight it was hidden behind trees. So was my nocturnal sight part of Bastien's venom? It was so easy to run, and I'm not exactly an athlete. Especially not traipsing through bogs and patches of smelly mud. I would have thought my boots would sink down and I'd get stuck. Instead, I was keeping up with Grey and Ivan was the one having trouble running.

The house loomed ahead of us as we burst out of the line of swampy woods. It was huge and well lit from inside. Though after a few seconds I realized the light was coming from dozens of Salamanders sailing through the air, hot on the heels of retreating robed Magicians. I saw Gnomes swinging axes and throwing rocks, Undines gathering water from the surrounding woods and causing waves of it to tumble unsuspecting Magicians ass over end into the swamp. A Sylph made of dark, black soot billowed through the front door of the house and spat out a few more robed bodies.

Dark blurs of movement preceded the echo of growls as Bastien's pack entered the almost comical scene. But whereas the Elementals toyed, teased and created mischief, the Lycans were drawing blood. The three of us stood on the precipice of precedent. This was insane. Dangerous. And just…wrong.

<I have found your friend!>

Grey and I heard Bastien at the same time and instinctually followed the link into the house. The smell of bog and wood permeated the place. It looked like an episode of *Elementals Gone Wild* as we maneuvered around screaming Magicians and over exuberant creatures. Grey picked her way down the hall of oak and turned right behind a staircase as the Rock Creature I'd seen earlier tumbled down the steps. I followed her into a room and then to the right down another flight of steps. The temperature dropped drastically as we descended. I took in the damp stone walls, as well as the rusting iron hooks on the wooden frame of the steps.

At the bottom was Bastien in all his Lycan glory. His fur gleamed in the flickering lights provided by several Salamanders that scurried along the wooden ceiling. The room itself was a good size, probably half the length and width of the antebellum above. But what I saw in the room creeped me out.

The first thing I thought of was Dr. Frankenstein's laboratory. The only thing missing was the monster and a lightning storm with electricity arcing from a bunch of metal towers. The gurney with the straps was ready, but something dark and still sticky coated most of the metal as well as the restraints. Metal shelves full of glass jars containing Goddess knows what lined the walls as fluorescent lights half hung from chains where they'd been bashed in and torn free.

In the corner was a metal cage and in that cage was Kyle. Grey and I ran to him with Bastien beside us. His wrists were locked in some weird board that kept them apart but locked in front of him. And the cage was locked. Kyle looked okay, if a bit dirty. I saw smudges on his face and I hoped like hell that was dirt too, because if they were bruises? I'd feed Circe to Bastien myself.

"She took Jack," Kyle said as I looked around for some way to break the lock. "And she took Marilla."

<I can sense Marilla was here, and Jack, but I still can't touch their minds.>

Ivan came down the steps and whistled. "Damn Kyle, you're really in a dungeon."

"Shut up and get me out of this."

Bastien's form blurred as he shifted back into a man. It sounded a lot worse than I remembered it, but that might be because we were all in a room with echoes. The sound of snapping bones was never pleasant. Once he was upright and smoothed his hair back, he faced Kyle. "Was Marilla alive?"

"Yeah, she was. But you didn't say she was *really* pregnant."

"I didn't lie."

"No, but you omitted that she's ready to pop."

Oh. I hesitated and looked up at Bastien very much aware he was naked. Again. His heat warmed me in the basement or lab or dungeon, whatever this was. It also drew me to him, as I realized I was unconsciously moving closer. "She's ready to have the baby?"

"Yes," he looked back at Kyle as I glanced back at Ivan picking his way to us. "Why did she take them?"

That's when I heard it in Kyle's voice. He was upset. And when I looked at him, I saw it in his face. I grabbed the bars. They were like ice to the touch. "What did she do?"

"She had him on that table. She carved into his skin. He was screaming...oh Goddess, Sam. I couldn't stand it. But I couldn't do anything," he held up his bound wrists. "Then she forced him to drink a potion, took Marilla and they left."

"How long ago?" Bastien asked.

"Several hours ago. I've been down here alone while they were partying upstairs."

I could only guess Circe had forced Jack to drink the same potion that had mutated those two innocents and turned Bastien's brother into a monster. This didn't bode well for Jack, and I could feel Kyle's heart break. The room filled with small specks of Arcane as I reached down and touched the lock holding the cage. My intent had been to make the lock disappear. Instead, the entire cage vanished. All of it.

After everyone's initial WTF moment, Bastien stepped forward and broke the wooden handcuffs on Kyle, pretty much cracking the wood into several pieces. Kyle rubbed his wrists as I held out my arms to him. He was cool against me and I felt him shiver.

When he pulled back he stared into my face. "Your skin's hot. The fever's started."

"*Oui*. Therefore, we must find Marilla," Bastien looked around. "Where is Arden?"

Ivan pointed to the ceiling, indicating the subtle sounds still audible where we were. "They're upstairs, ransacking the place. As far as I can tell, the Magicians are all incapacitated, probably bleeding from wolf bites."

"The bites will heal fast. Then they will seek me out." He turned and in a second blur, bounded up the stairs in wolf form.

"What does he mean?" Kyle asked.

I filled him in on what Arden and the pack had done as we started toward the stairs. He didn't like what he heard, but he wasn't as upset about it as I was. And I think if it'd been me, having just spent nearly twenty-four hours as a prisoner locked up in a cage, I wouldn't feel as bad about their fate either.

Kyle turned away from us at that moment and looked at the shelves. He grabbed a few bottles and jars off, plucked a black bag from the rubble and piled everything in. "Let's go."

"Do you know where she took them?" I asked as we went back up the steps, Grey ahead of us and Ivan behind.

"No. She never made sense when she talked."

We stepped out into a gathering of Witches in the hallway. They were Arden's coven. They were laughing and talking, excited and all clutching things. They were magical looters bent on destruction.

Arden came around the staircase. Clutched in her hands were a bow, a quiver and one arrow. They were gold and gleamed under the light of several Salamanders. "It's time to leave. Bastien said you got Kyle?"

Kyle waved at his aunt. And to my surprise, she pushed her way through the milling Witches and embraced her nephew. I think that was the first time I'd ever seen that happen, given they didn't have the smoothest relationship. I took a closer look at the quiver, arrow and bow, touched them and yanked my hand back fast.

They were ice cold. "Arden…what is that?" I needed to know.

"It's one of the stolen artifacts I mentioned," she said it quickly. "We've scanned the house. The Codex isn't here." She looked around at everyone as if counting.

Kyle looked at the quiver. "What good is it with only one arrow?"

"I'm only going to need one arrow," Arden raised her hand. The talking stopped and all eyes were on her. Even the Elementals were paying attention. "Friends, Witches, Elementals, our harvest here was good and our ritual is done. We bid farewell to the Watchtowers of the East. May you go in peace and tranquility."

The Sylphs all vanished with happy smiles and laughter. I watched her dismiss each of the Elements, thanking them, and then I felt something very cold touch my hand. When I looked down my Undine was sitting on the edge of the quiver, and she was shaking her head at it and pointing. But before I could get more from her, Arden dismissed Watchtowers of the West and she was gone with a bubble pop.

My Undine had come to this ritual in that jar, and she'd somehow participated in this and then showed her dislike for the artifact in Arden's grasp. I had no explanation of any of it. No frame of reference to infer. In this, I was lost.

"Everyone, the Alpha and his pack have departed in search of their sister and unborn child. We have sworn to help them, and we shall. I need my quarters to gather your teams and meet back at Gypsy Gardens. We have until dawn to find them."

When everyone dispersed, I touched Arden's shoulder. The face she turned to me was blank. Almost…alien. "I'm not sure why she wants the girl wolf. Why not just leave her here? She's got the Codex."

"The Codex is a spell, you know that."

"Yeah."

"And what do spells need to work?"

I thought about that and of course came up with my mom's standard answer. "A spell is verbal, it's material and it needs focus." These things translated into a spoken chant, the ingredients needed to infuse the spell, and the caster's focus or will.

"She has the spell, she has the focus. She needs the material. The spell is an Arcane spell, Sam. What component do Arcane spells require that we as the God Mother's children abhor?"

I had the answer. A life. A death. Taken in the moment.

Arden said, "Wolves know when their children will be born. This child comes at dawn. If we don't find them, I'm afraid Circe will take that child, and kill it to fulfill that spell."

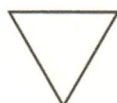

TWENTY TWO

I didn't want to go to Gypsy Gardens, and as long as I had my guys with me, I wasn't going to. Everyone agreed to head to the shop, to our base of power, so to speak. Getting there was the worst part because all I had was Ivan's truck. Ivan and Grey volunteered to ride in the back and I was very, very careful about my driving. I didn't want to hit a hole and knock them into the road, and I didn't want to draw attention to us because I wasn't really sure if this was legal.

It was just after two when we pulled into the back and got inside. I sent Kyle upstairs to take a shower. Luckily, he kept clothing in the shop for those nights he went from work to the clubs to have a cocktail. Ivan, Grey and I stayed in the break room and I set my unused bag on the tabletop. It was still open from when I'd removed the glass jar so I started pulling things from inside and set them on the table. The bag is where I put Fred's gun. The gun is what I was looking for.

But the gun wasn't there.

I fished around inside of the bag with my hand and when I still didn't find it, I turned it upside down. Bits and pieces of paper and dirt and a penny fell out. But no gun. Panicked, I went back outside to the truck and tore it apart looking for Fred's firearm. But it wasn't there.

"What are you looking for?" Ivan said as he showed up on the opposite side of his truck.

"Something I had in my bag when I left it near that rock. But now it's not inside."

"You left it there when you went inside the house."

I had. Because I'd forgotten about it once I realized Bastien's pack was biting Magicians. The only reason I remembered it on the way back was because I spotted it beside the rock. Crap. Maybe the gun fell out in the woods. Had I rubbed it down good enough? Could they tell it had been in my apartment? Or had someone taken it out of my bag?

"Sam?"

I put my hand to my cheek. My skin was so hot and I thought I smelled Bastien. It was sudden, like a forgotten perfume caught in the breeze. The scent of leaves and earth. I started shivering as my knees gave out. Ivan moved fast and grabbed me under my shoulders. "Damn…is it the venom?"

I nodded as I used him to climb back up to my feet and then leaned on him as we went back inside. In the break room he made me tea as Kyle came down the stairs. He looked much better, but I could see the red marks on his wrists made by the wooden shackles.

"What happened?"

Ivan nodded at me. "The venom. We've got maybe five hours, tops, before she shifts and there's no way out."

"No," Kyle said. "We've got more time than that." He moved around the table and picked up the bag he'd taken from Circe's and set it on the table next to the mess I'd made of my own bag. We watched as he set out each jar and bottle and then moved to a shelf beside the door where he kept his tools. There he grabbed a mortar and pestle, a bowl, a small cauldron, candles and a cup. He placed each of the items on the table and started mixing things into the mortar from the jars and bottles.

"What are you doing? We don't have time to make potions right now."

"I have time." Kyle continued working, talking sometimes as he drew symbols in the air periodically.

I could see the colors and I had an idea of what he was doing. "You know the cure."

"I was paying attention. I know the properties of roots, herbs, flowers and plants. I saw what she did and I've been working on a remedy, a counter potion to hers. I don't know if it'll work, but I have to try to save Jack."

"Maybe it won't change him," I said. "Bastien told me he and the others drank the potion in the house and they didn't change."

"Bastien didn't change because he's not apogee. He's a full blood."

"But wasn't his brother full blood?" Ivan asked. "André. The one that changed."

"No." Kyle continued to work as he spoke, but I could feel the stress radiating off of him. I could also feel his exhaustion. "They weren't blood brothers. Bastien created André and they became brothers. André was apogee. Marilla is perigee, that's why they hope the baby will be born perigee." He reached over to the pile of bottles and jars and hesitated. Kyle balled that hand in to a fist and sighed. "This just isn't going to work."

"Why? What do you need?"

"What I need—I don't think it exists." Kyle looked at Ivan and I as Grey's claws clacked on the hardwood floor. "I was basing this idea off of the Iliad. Just because Circe seemed very taken with the idea that she was actually Circe."

Ivan frowned but I knew where he was going. Magic did indeed work more on intent of will and belief than by any other means. Even my Elementals couldn't perform what they did if I didn't believe in them. And they in turn received their orders from my want, my goal, my outcome, which I always visualized. So if Olivia Graham really believed she was Circe from legend, then she would know about moly and how Odysseus used it to evade her magic. So she would believe such an herb would defeat her magic. "And?"

"And…Sam you know how it works. Eighty percent of potions and magic works off of intent and belief. If she believed she was really Circe, then I need to create this with moly."

"Moly?" Ivan poured himself a cup of tea. "Is that a plant or a herb?"

"Ivan, have you read the Iliad?" I smiled at him.

"Yeah, but that was like, back in school. And I think I slept through most of it."

I patted his hand. "Circe is the Witch that turned Odysseus's men into swine by having them drink a potion. The only way Odysseus escaped this fate was because Hermes gave him the herb moly to eat."

Ivan's eyes widened. "And we all know some truths are hidden in myths. So, where do we get moly?"

"It doesn't exist." Kyle's shoulders slumped and he sat down hard on one of the chairs. "That's the one thing I didn't really think through. There's no such thing."

Yes there is.

I sat back and looked down at Grey. "It's real?"

Ivan and Kyle looked at me.

Yes it is. Or really, it's what we believe is moly.

I leaned in toward her. "And that is…"

140

Snowdrop.

"Snowdrop?"

Kyle slapped his hands on the table. "What is that?"

But Ivan was already on it. He had his hands out, moving barely visible web pages in the air. Google boy at work. "Snowdrop. It's also known as galanthus. It's a small offshoot of bulbous herbaceous plants in the family of amaryllidaceae. Most flower in winter before the vernal equinox and some species can bloom in spring and late autumn."

That's it.

"Dammit. Where am I going to get any of that now? It's after two in the morning and I'm pretty sure no one's going to know what it is."

I know where there's some.

I closed my eyes. I already knew what she was going to say. "It's growing at Ina's house, isn't it? In Ina's garden?"

Yes. I saw it there when we were there before. I thought it was odd she had it planted but it's in the north quadrant.

Kyle was on his feet. "Is it really at Ina's house?"

"Grey says it is. She saw it there." I did *not* want to go back to Ina's house. I mean I really didn't want to. The idea of going back to that house knowing there were all those dead people buried in the back yard just gave me the creeps. But I couldn't really tell people that. I couldn't tell anyone. And I sure as hell didn't want the local police to start digging it all up.

But Kyle was already packing his stuff back into that bag. "Let's go. I can finish it there."

"Kyle, we don't even know where Circe took Marilla and Jack. Bastien's got his whole pack searching the city and I haven't heard a word." And that scared me. I felt like I needed to be searching myself, but I was so tired, and so cold, and aching all over my body. Not even Ivan's tea was helping.

"Then let's just go over there and get it so I can at least try something. Maybe on the way they'll contact you through that link or something."

The bodies aren't going to come out of the ground and hurt you, Sam-Sam.

"That's not what spooks me," I said aloud but I was making myself stand. "It's just the idea they're there."

"What's there?"

"Never mind. Let's go. I'll call Arden and see if they know anything."

"Let's take my car," Kyle said as we went to the door. "It'll fit more people. We should swing by and grab your Jeep on the way there."

I was pulling out my phone while I nodded and thumbed through the numbers. I saw Crwys's number and paused over it as we piled into the Prius. I wanted to call him, make sure he was okay and still mending. I also noticed I had five missed calls from Prescott. Let her fucking hang. Bitch took my mom.

Grey crawled in the back with me and I leaned into her for warmth as I called Arden. It went straight to voicemail. "Hey Arden. It's Sam. We're running by Ina's to pick up something. Please call if your people or Bastien finds them."

Once I hung up, I shoved the phone back into my jeans pocket and leaned back to close my eyes. I could hear the pack now, a cacophony of voices over the air. Each of them reporting back to the whole. They couldn't find them. And without my Elementals, I didn't think I could Track the way my mom used to.

My muscles ached as I shivered. I couldn't do this on my own. I was gonna need help. And I was gonna need it fast. I pulled the phone out again and texted the one person I knew who could possibly find a renegade Magician.

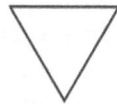

TWENTY THREE

Ina's house was lit up. This was my first clue something was wrong because no one lived there. It'd been empty since Dionysus absconded with my aunt's body, the body he'd been puppeting since I was eight years old, and fled the area. I didn't know if he'd fled the country and if I ever saw him again, I wouldn't blink twice at doing to him what I did to Fred.

Was it possible he was back in town and Ina was back in her house? I hoped somehow if that were true, I'd know it. Maybe some seventh sense or something.

We sat in Kyle's Prius, in front of Ina's house where I always got a parking spot. It was an old spell Ina had cast on the area just for me. The spell would always work as long as I continued to park there occasionally. All four of us stared at the house.

"So…" Kyle began. "Anyone got any ideas?"

"Not really." My teeth chattered from shaking. I was trying really hard to pull it together but the chills that set in during the drive over weren't something I could control no matter how warm the scar on my chest became. I assumed it was reacting to my emotional anxiety. "I'm not sure I want to know who's in there."

"I have to get the snowdrop," Kyle said as he shrugged his backpack on. "I'm not giving up on Jack. Not like this."

A harsh knock against the driver's side window made us all jump. A person dressed in a black robe and hood stood outside of the door, wielding the toughest and most powerful magic known to mankind.

A Glock 9mm.

The figure stepped back and gestured for us to get out of the Prius with his free hand. Everyone glanced at each other, all silently

143

asking what we were going to do, even though we each opened up our prospective doors. I stood to the side in the chilled night air and waited for Grey to jump out to the sidewalk.

"Hello," Kyle said to the hooded gunman. "Can we help you?"

"Inside. All of you." The voice was male and didn't click any memory bells. He stood back as we all filed in line behind one another and walked down walkway to Ina's front door.

There was a time I thought I knew this house as well as I knew myself. I had lived here with Ina since I was fourteen. I helped her upgrade the bathrooms, the kitchen and I helped her plant the garden. What I did not help her with were the bodies buried in the back.

Circe met us at the door, her hands clasped in front of her. A small part of me half expected, in a terrified sort of way, to see Inamorata standing beside the Magician. But Ina wasn't there. Ina was far away from New Orleans. We paused just inside the door in the foyer as the gunman closed the door and locked it.

The tall, half-blurred face of Olivia Graham took in each of us. Her gaze fixed on Grey and she frowned. "That's a real wolf."

"She's a dog." I know I shouldn't have said anything, but that was my go-to defense when anyone remarked about Grey. "Well, she's half Husky, half Labrador."

"But she's a real canine. Not a shifter."

I looked at Grey who looked up at me. *She can't tell I'm a paladin. Her limited magic won't reveal the real me.*

The real you? I made a face at her, not quite sure what that meant, so I put asking more questions on the back burner.

"Put the dog in the mud room and lock the door."

"No!" It slipped out as the gunman started toward Grey and I slipped between them. "She's my familiar. I need her with me."

"Then all the more reason to keep her away from you. Gydion, put her in the mud room."

Grey growled as the gunman named Gydion grabbed the fur and skin on the back of her neck, but I quieted her down with the reassurance I'd be back to let her out soon as I could. My anxiety level rose as I watched her being half dragged away and I felt the mark sear my chest. I put a hand over it and felt the heat through my shirt.

"It's so nice to see you again," the Magician said as she turned and headed into the house. Two more robed men with their hoods down flanked us as they ushered us to follow Circe. I fell in between

Kyle and Ivan, with Ivan's hand on my shoulder. "I must say I was very impressed with the way you handled my spectres."

"What are you doing in Inamorata's house?" I had to ask, and I made sure to do it once we were through the dining room, heading to the open sliding glass doors. The house looked fine. Nothing broken or stolen.

She paused in the doorway and turned. I didn't much care for the look on her face. "Let's not play coy, Miss Hawthorne. You already know I was friends with Inamorata. I have a key to this place, and I know more about its hidden secrets than you."

As she turned to head out the door, I couldn't stop myself. I didn't like her and I was feeling very aggressive. The edges of my vision were tinged with red, sparkly power waiting for me to give it permission to destroy. And that realization frightened me more than anything. Would there be a day when it wouldn't wait for my permission and I would be the one watching from the edges as it wreaked its destructive power?

"You mean the secrets like the bodies? The deaths she used to create the Coyote Flame?"

Circe's back went rigid as she straightened her arms down at her sides. She obviously didn't like being one-upped and the bodies were a sticky secret.

"Oh…I get it." I stepped forward and Ivan's hand slipped off my shoulder. "You helped her kill those people, didn't you? That's how you know who I am. So, part of you is connected to that doorway, isn't it?"

I'd moved past Kyle as I spoke and stood directly in front of her. She turned fast, but I expected it. Or a sudden surge in my senses expected it. I knew she was going to strike and when she moved, it was in slow motion. I grabbed her striking wrist and held it between us. We were close to the same height—Circe had about an inch or two on me.

One of the gunmen stepped forward and slammed his fist down my arm. It hurt. I let go of Circe's wrist, snarled at the bastard and grabbed the gunman's forearm.

He disappeared in a swirl of black and red mist that smelled faintly of blood and smoke.

Kyle and Ivan both backed up. I felt them pull away as my shaking intensified. I was so, so cold and yet I could feel my skin crawling with heat. I looked at my outstretched hand. Arcane power popped and sparkled just beneath my skin like lightning within a thundercloud. Circe took two steps back, pulled her hands back and took off running into the center of the garden. The other gunman backed up as well as I turned and looked at him and said, "Boo."

He ran in the opposite direction toward the front door. I heard it slam on his way out.

When I looked at Kyle and Ivan my heart dropped into my already knotted stomach. Their eyes were wide and their fists up in front of them. Ivan's glowed brilliant green and Kyle's were blue and yellow. I looked between the two of them, shivering, then turned and looked back to the garden.

Circe was in the center of the Circle Ina and I had created years ago. Any Cowen looking to the back would just see a circular garden, with concentric circles of flowers planted in four quarters. But the magically inclined would see the significance and the base for a ritual space. It was the place where I'd killed Arwen at Samhain, and where Arden and her coven had opened the Coyote Flame and freed the Changeling children in December.

And here we were, back again a third time, with another bad guy threatening to do bad things to an innocent. I could see a girl lying on the ground in the center of the stone circle where the fire pit was. I could also see the swell of her belly where a child slept in anticipation of birth. And I could see the mother wasn't moving.

I glanced behind me at the two of them. "You two can stand there and look at me like I'm some kind of monster or you can get your asses out there and help me save Jack, Marilla and her baby. Kyle, free Grey from the mud room and she can show you where the snowdrop is." Whether or not they decided to help me, having just seen me obliterate a man, didn't matter. The only thing I could see was the girl, the baby and a Magician that needed to be put down.

So I took off running to that Circle, calling every ounce of Arcane I had at my fingertips, ready to get rid of this bitch for good.

Something grabbed my ankle in mid run. I wasn't running that fast. I had a fever that would probably send any thermometer into a fit and my muscles ached as if on fire, so I wasn't all that surprised that something caught me. What I didn't expect to see after I slammed into the damp, wet ground and bit dirt, was a bony, skeletal hand. It sprang out of the ground, pushing dirt and plugs of grass to the sides as it held my ankle in a vice-like grip.

The ground around it rippled and shot up as the rest of the body popped up like broken bones through skin. I screamed.

Ivan appeared at my side, stomping on the femur connected to the hand with his sneakers. The bones broke but the hand continued its death grip on my ankle. My Cyber Witch dropped to the ground where I sat staring at the skeletal hand on my boot and started pulling and yanking at the finger bones. "Damn! Sam! This is one of those bodies, isn't it?"

"Yes!"

I reached out and gingerly touched the knuckle of one bone and the whole hand disappeared in a poof of black smoke.

Ivan helped me to my feet as the entire garden moved and shifted. More bodies erupted from the earth and pulled their rotted selves out of the earth.

I pointed at them as I grabbed Ivan's arm. He flinched, but when he realized I wasn't going to make him disappear in a cloud of smoke he grabbed my arm back. "We got *zombies!*"

"No shit!" It was obvious Ivan didn't know what to do. His Gift dealt with Cyber Magic, and this was way outside his wheelhouse. "What do we do?"

I looked around at the bodies as they all turned at once and faced us. Just past them were Grey and Kyle on the other side of the Circle digging in the ground. No one had seemed to notice them yet, and there were more of them than us. Keeping their attention away from Kyle and Grey was the better idea.

I pulled him to the house. "We run!"

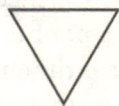

TWENTY FOUR

I wasn't in good shape. And it was obvious as I stumbled against Ivan and he worked to get his arm underneath my shoulder. I cursed Ina for having such a huge back yard as we neared the house, only to be blocked by one of the monsters. This zombie was still half dressed, with a yellow t-shirt, bits and pieces of jeans and yellowish hair. I recognized him as Bill, one of the last homeless guys Ina took in before I left for college.

He was fresher so he was faster and grabbed Ivan's hoodie. Ivan started hacking way with a very poor imitation of Kung-Fu. I reached out to make this one disappear like the others.

Only he didn't. Not immediately. He started smoking and moving in a jerky motion as bits and pieces of him caught fire and smoldered like glowing embers. It slowed him down but it didn't destroy him. Ivan took that chance, pulled his arm away—actually Bill's arm came with us—and we ran past him back into the house.

Ivan slammed the door shut and pried the still moving zombie hand off his arm and slammed it onto the tile where he promptly started stomping on it.

One of the doors opened and I turned at a dizzying speed. But it was just Kyle and Grey coming in. "They're right behind me."

I put my hand on my forehead. It was so hot. Was it possible for skin to be this hot and not set itself on fire? "Up the stairs. Ina's room is probably the safest. It's in the back and gives a good view of the back garden."

"Sam, are you okay?" Ivan asked as he pulled me to him and we started up the stairs.

"No. I'm not. But we can't worry about this."

It's starting. You need the antidote.

Yeah, Mom, no kidding.

We made it up the steps and into Ina's room. Nothing had changed inside. Everything looked as it did before, as if life had been interrupted. I sat on the edge of the bed, Ivan locked the door and pulled the chair from the dresser and wedged it under the doorknob as Kyle and Grey went to the window.

"What the hell is she doing?" Kyle asked.

"I have no idea. I don't understand the workings of a crazy Magician."

Ivan moved from the door and put his hand on my forehead. "You're burning up. Maybe that's why that weird magic didn't work."

I was thinking that myself. Grey was oddly quiet and I nudged her mind. She sent back a stream of love and adoration. She was just worried about how to save Marilla.

"About that—" Kyle started.

I held up my hand. "Not now. I don't know. Just get your potion made. We don't have time for arguing."

He did as I suggested, though I could feel the worry, hesitation and fear radiating off of him as he cleared off the dresser and set out the things he needed. Doors broke downstairs and I looked at Ivan. That didn't sound like slow moving zombies. That was something bashing into the doors from the garden.

I looked outside at the Circle where Circe stood over Marilla. She wasn't at the door. With a glance at Ivan, I went to he door, carefully unlocked it and peeked out.

At the other end of the hall appeared—the only way I can describe it is if someone were to take a wolf, a yeti, and André the Giant and combine their DNA. It was big and hunched over and stood up on its back haunches like a man, but it was covered in glossy black fur. Its arms stuck out in front, reaching for things. Its talons raked along the dry wall, pulling up long gouges as it turned in the hall and looked right at me.

Sweet Lord and Lady Darksome!

I squealed like a little girl, slammed the door and locked it.

"What?" Ivan said.

I looked at Kyle. He had his small cauldron going with a tiny fire inside and was holding a beaker over it with a pair of tongs and in his hand was the snowdrop. "What?" he said to me. "Is it Jack?"

I wasn't sure, but I was heavy on the maybe. So I nodded. "Kyle, I don't know how in the hell you plan on getting him to drink that."

"Answer me," Kyle stood and started toward me. "Is it Jack?"

I put my hand up. "Just finish!"

That's when the first slam against the door happened. The wood in the door cracked, the frame split, but it didn't open immediately. I turned and put my hand on the door and imagined it made of steel. Sparkling red covered the door and melted into the wood, creating something different. I just didn't know what. Jack smashed against it again and I was pretty sure he was body slamming it in his attempt to get to us. The new door didn't budge.

Kyle hesitated but he turned back to the little setup on the dresser and I watched as he lowered the snowdrop plant into the beaker. There was an instant reaction as the liquid turned bright red and then blue and then smoke billowed up and out over the beaker's edge as the potion settled on a dull orange. And the smell?

Like wild onions.

"Is that it?" I pointed to the smoking beaker.

"Yes. I'm just not sure how to get it into him."

I stared at it. "Will it work on me?"

Kyle glanced at the flask. "I don't know."

Sam... Grey's voice had a warning note.

"Mom, don't. Bastien's not here. I can't even feel him through the pack link because my mind's just a jumble of worries and random thoughts as this fever eats away at it. We found Marilla. She's out there. And I'm going to need to be full strength to fight that crazy woman."

Kyle and Ivan looked between my mom and I as Jack continued banging on the door.

"Sam, the door might hold, but the wall around it won't," Ivan pointed out.

I stepped back and looked. Sure enough, the drywall around the door was cracking as dust fell from breaks in the ceiling. He was right. I gave it another three good slams before it all came down.

"Here," Kyle thrust the flask in my face. "You use it. You're right. We're going to need that seriously messed up magic of yours to get out of this and protect that baby."

I stared at the flask and then looked at Kyle's face.

Some say our eyes are the windows to our souls. I've always considered that a pick-up line. Until I looked into Kyle's eyes that day. They weren't as dark as I'd always thought they were. His eyes were a mixture of colors, but mostly green, gold and brown. All of that amounted to hazel. But it was the impression of emotion that overwhelmed me looking into his eyes. I saw desperation, I saw despair and worry, I saw fear and I saw…love. I didn't know if apogee wolves could force a link the way Bastien had on me, but I did sense their relationship had matured deeper than anything Kyle had ever felt before.

All of his life, Kyle had fought for acceptance. Acceptance for being gay, acceptance for being the only male Hedge Witch in the Vervain family. Acceptance within himself for what the God Mother gave to him. And now he'd found someone seeking that same acceptance. A young man with a wolf's curse seeking acceptance and Kyle was willing, ready and thoroughly able to give it.

In that second my eyes locked with his, I knew there was no way I could sacrifice Jack's only chance at living a life with Kyle. There was enough potion for both of us—that much I was sure of—having tried several of Kyle's brews. And this potion was super charged not only with the power of its roots, herbs and plants, but with the desire and belief it would give Jack back to him.

A slam against the door caused the frame to crack inward. I felt the door shift against me. One more hit like that to the door and the big bad wolf was going to blow the house down. I had one chance and if I screwed it up, Jack would tear me apart, and then he'd go after my boys.

I couldn't let that happen.

I faced the door, but I moved to the side so when the door fell in, it wouldn't crush me underneath it. I held the flask in front of me and concentrated on the glass. If I could make a body vanish, why not make the glass vanish? Or something even better, why couldn't I transmute it into a container of air? Something that I could grasp without worrying about cutting Jack or myself. My shaking wasn't helping, or the fact my knees shook. I didn't know if this was from abject terror or the wolf fever.

And then the door came down and I didn't have time to think anymore. Jack loomed big, loud and in full stereo in front of us as he came through the door. At that moment, I realized any idea I might have come up with was heading out the window like paper caught in a strong gust of wind. Instinct and the need to protect my bacon, as well as Ivan's and Kyle's, became the singular thought.

I couldn't fight this behemoth as it came through the door. I wasn't strong enough to wrestle it to the ground and pour the potion in its mouth. My imagination and my over exuberant positive attitude really hadn't thought this one through.

As he swung at me, I ducked and moved behind him. That left the boys vulnerable and in Jack's line of sight. I had to think in seconds of something that could stop him and help me! If Jack's human mind were in control, I could just reason with him to be quiet and let me pour it down. He'd thank me later.

Be quiet…and still.

I didn't think about how I would do it. Nor did I spare a moment to consider what I was thinking wouldn't work. Holding the flask in one hand I reached out with the other and touched Jack's back with the thought of him freezing in place. When he suddenly stopped moving, I knew it'd worked so I looked at Kyle. "Take the flask and pour it down his throat. Hurry!"

Kyle scrambled around Jack's unmoving form to get the flask, and once he had it I watched him run back around. I saw determination in his expression as he pushed up on Jack's elongated snout, shoved the long cylindrical end of the flask between Jack's sharp teeth and poured it down. Some of it spilled over but it didn't matter as long as some of it went in.

As for me, the strain of keeping the Arcane power focused was a battle I was losing. My muscles felt like they needed oiling as I moved and I was losing the strength to stand. Wavering from the intent worried me as I felt my eyes close. Exhaustion paired with the venom zapped my strength and I didn't know if I was going to be able to stop Circe. This might be one fight I'll have to sleep through.

"Sam!"

I jerked up and looked at Kyle.

"Sam let go!"

But I couldn't. When I tried to pull my hand away I discovered it was covered in ice. In fact, Jack's lower half was being quickly encased in ice!

"Sam you have to let go!" Ivan was at my side.

"I…I can't." I wasn't strong enough. The Arcane was happy doing what it did best—causing chaos. And it wasn't listening to what I wanted. I stopped trying to pull my hand free as I my eyes closed again and this time I was pulled down by the lull of the Arcane.

-*Such a monster shouldn't exist.*-

No…it shouldn't.

-And we have the power to stop it. We have the power to take that woman down as well. We can stop all of the evil. Make it all go away.-

Yeah…make it all go away.

I knew I was half hanging off of Jack's back, my hand in ice with Ivan and Kyle yelling. Or talking. I couldn't tell. My body shook as I succumbed to that voice. I was so tired and it wanted control. It wanted to do the work for me while I rested. It wanted to treat me like the Queen I was.

<A Queen are we?> came Bastien's snort in my mind as voices whispered to me. *<No Queen of mine kills indifferently.>*

<<Your Queen? She's my Queen.>>

Crwys! How was he chiming in on the pack link?

And then he was there, his mind brushing against my own, his magic cradling mine. I felt the Arcane pitch, buckle and protest its control being taken, but as it had when I had my Elementals, his magic was now guiding my new power and forcing it to do my will. I heard people talking, I heard whispers and I heard…

"Sam? Please, baby. I need you to open your eyes."

I did and found his amber red peepers looking down at me. I followed the crease of his eyelids, to the arch of his brows. The slope of his nose was enticing and I wanted to lick it before I kissed his sensual, pouty lips.

"She's smiling."

"That's great. Now get her up. We have to go down there and stop Circe!"

That was Ivan. I was cradled in Crwys's arms and he was so warm. I didn't want to move. But he pulled me up and into a sitting position so I could see the room. Jack was on his side, naked, his eyes closed, but no longer a monster. He looked as human as he ever had. Kyle pulled the duvet off the bed and covered his lover with it before he rested Jack's head in his lap.

Ivan moved to the window to look out as Bastien accompanied him. "She's still down there with Marilla. But I can't see what she's doing. What the hell does she want?"

<<She wants the baby's essence, the very thing that will make it perigee. She believes this will cement the Arcane spell.>>

I pushed away and Crwys and I stood. "She's going to kill both Marilla and the baby. We can't let that happen."

<The pack is ready and waiting.>

"But what about the zombies?"

Crwys led me to the window. I put my hand against the glass and watched the shadows of those Ina and Circe murdered for their foul magic. I didn't have the strength to run around the place zapping zombies into nothing, and if that last zombie was any example of my remaining strength? I'd just piss them all off by singeing them.

Abruptly, every moving shadow lit up like a roman candle and then disappeared. The whole scene reminded me of the day in the park when Dionysus's Ghouls ignited and went up in flames. I looked at Crwys and grinned at him.

"What zombies?"

I put my hand on his cheek. "I love you."

"I know," he grabbed my hand and entwined his fingers with mine. "LeBlanc, I need your pack flanking the garden. Keep her separated from anything or anyone else she might call in."

The big red wolf nodded.

"Ivan, you get on the net and see if you can bring in some help just in case we need it."

"Who?"

"Arden for one. Find out where the hell she is."

"Roger."

He looked at Kyle. "You stay here with Jack. Make sure he's okay."

And then he looked at me. "Ready to go kick some Ceremonial ass together?"

"Roger."

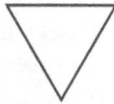

TWENTY FIVE

We proceeded cautiously down the stairs. Mentally, I felt a bit more confident with Crwys beside me. Having Bastien and his pack there was also a big boost to the "yay for our team" side of things. Physically was a whole other state of being. I was in a full on fever now, and I moved in a sort of dreamlike state as Crwys held on to me. We walked through the sliding glass doors to the garden. Ina's beautifully tended grass was destroyed, marred by chunks of earth and roots. Or I hoped they were roots because they sort of looked like bones protruding up from the destroyed ground.

The house floodlights were on, illuminating the mess as we stood at the garden's edge. Circe stood in the center with Marilla at her feet. Did anyone even know if the wolf was still alive? It didn't look like she'd moved since we got there.

The pack appeared from the shadows, fifteen large, magnificent wolves in all. A powerful pallet of gray, brown, black, white and red. None was as big as Bastien who stood to my left. The garden no longer smelled of flowers, but of musk and freshly turned earth. With Crwys's arm holding me up, we walked across that mutilated ground toward Circe. I jumped at every noise; afraid another body Crwys missed was going to jump up and grab me again, and I was pretty sure I didn't have the strength to make it go away.

Circe watched us, and I noticed the smug expression on her face. She didn't think we were a threat, but an audience to watch her grand finale.

The circle contracted until it surrounded the stone circle. From this distance, I could see Marilla breathing. She wasn't tied down or anything, but she wasn't trying to get free. Her face was turned away so I couldn't tell if she was awake or unconscious.

"Interesting trick, Detective. I've only ever read about such control of fire, but I have never seen it. I think you are going to make an interesting addition to my army."

"Army?" I blurted that one out. All through this I had been looking for some kind of realistic, reasonable motive for her to be doing what she was doing. Crwys and Levi had taught me about motives, about what drives us to act a certain way and I got that. I understood Dionysus's motive to create the Changelings to drive Medbh's location into the open. I didn't agree with it, but I understood it. I understood Dionysus destroying Inamorata's life to survive. I understood Kennett's motive to seek out revenge on those he perceived were a threat to him and his continued existence after finding his body dead. Or Bastien's need to save the unborn baby by biting me and making me a part of the pack, which was going to be a permanent state of being if I didn't get this show on the road.

To some, motives may seem trivial. But by understanding a monster's reasoning, their kryptonite could be found. Sometimes.

Circe was looking at me. It was a weird look. "Yes. My army."

"What, you plan on taking over the world or something?" Levi asked as he appeared across the way between two large black wolves. "Gonna…make yourself a little army of yeti or something?"

She glanced back at him and sneered. "I wouldn't expect a mere Vampire to understand the expectations and dreams of a Ceremonial Magician. But Samantha knows what I seek. She and I are kin, she and I are of the same mind!."

"Screw that!" I nearly growled at her. "I don't want to bring Arcane into the world!"

Circe held out her arms, palms up. "But it's not just that, Samantha! I want to rid the world of the God Mother's children completely. Don't you see? The Faerie had it right—to destroy the children is to free the borders once again. To open the gates, the Cairns and the doors so that Arcane can be the one true magic of this plane, as it is of other planes," she raised her arms as if punctuating her dream. "I will give Arcane to the Ceremonial Magicians!"

Crickets pretty much filled the silence after her declaration. I looked up at Crwys. "Can she do that?"

He shook his head. "Naw. That would take access to certain Thrones and a lot of ritual and a few spells." He shook his head.

"Nevermind! I'm afraid this crazy bitch doesn't have a VIP pass. The worst she can do right now is hurt Marilla and the baby."

I nodded in agreement.

Given the number of big wolves in addition to us, I didn't see how she thought she was going to survive. Then she held up a scroll of something. Looked like it had writing on it. "I have the Codex that will bring Arcane to the Magicians of the world!"

Crwys held out his hand and snapped his fingers. The scroll caught fire. Circe screamed and tossed the scroll away where it flew like a fireball and landed in one of the deeper pits of the garden grass.

"How dare you!"

Oh…shit. I had to side with Circe on this one. I glared at him. "You idiot! I needed that! Remember?"

Crwys put his hand his mouth and arched his brows. "Oops?" He said when he pulled his hand away. "Sorry."

I felt Circe gather her Arcane. My own reacted to hers, but not in a good way. More of a long time rival way. Like *Mean Girls*. Mine poured out from my hands as it formed a barrier of sparkling red light. Circe's power coalesced into a sphere around her and Marilla. I caught the flash of a knife just as Crwys did.

Just as the pack did.

"No!" I heard myself shout as we all started toward the center of the Circle at a dead run. The pack roared as it moved as one. I tried to stretch my magic out, extend it like an arm out to the Circle to stop the blade.

But no amount of speed was going to stop Circe from plunging that knife into Marilla's stomach. I saw the blood as it sprayed Circe's face and shot out over the girl's shirt. The pack screamed in my head as voices threatened to incapacitate me by their sheer volume. The part of me I sent out twisted as it built speed and knocked the blade from Circe's hand. She looked up at me, hissed and threw her own black Arcane at me. It fanned out around us and rose like a black sun above just before it shot its rays out to grab hold of every moving thing. Ropes of it entwined around the barrel chests of wolves and lifted them in the air. Their cries of agony told me those ropes weren't just holding them, but crushing them as well.

I heard Crwys cry out as well as Ivan and turned to see several of the ropes wrapping around Ivan's chest. Crwys's cry wasn't because he was trapped as the wolves were, but because he'd slipped his arms around Ivan to take some of the brunt of the vice-like grip.

Go!

I felt my mom's pain at that moment as it came through our connection. She was also in the throws of agony as that black sun crushed her chest.

-Listen to her. We can take this one. Just let us work for you. Let us eliminate her as we eliminated the animal.-

I knew the voice spoke of Fred. It viewed Fred as an animal.

I turned back to Circe. She stood with her arms out again, laughing as her black sun destroyed her enemies. She wasn't paying attention to me. I doubted she even realized I wasn't being crushed.

Why was that?

-We are protecting you.-

We?

-We will always protect you against all of your enemies. Let go.-

I wanted to let go. I wanted to take a hot bath and curl up in a warm bed and sleep. I'd gone beyond chills as my body temperature rose. I was now into the beginning stages of the shift. I didn't have much time left and there was no time for the antidote. I could feel my teeth sharpening and my skin crawling. I itched.

The wolf wanted out and Circe had to be stopped. Why not give in? Just let the shift happen and embrace the power of being a Lycan? Then I could rip her apart piece by piece and enjoy it.

No.

That wasn't Grey's voice. That was Crwys. *How—?*

Because we're a part of each other. It's so rare I have these feelings for a human, especially someone as troublesome as you. But when I mate, sweet Samantha, I mate for life.

There was something very odd about his mental voice. It sounded like his spoken voice, but there was a bass-like rumble. I didn't understand.

You have help. Use it. Touch my mind for strength, and don't give in to the Arcane voices.

How did he know about the voices? Did I tell him? I couldn't remember anything anymore. So when I looked for this help, I actively looked outside of my self and I found it. She was there, sitting on the edge of a particularly deep hole to my right, against the stones of the Circle.

My Undine.

She pointed at the hole. The bottom was filled with water. I looked at the black sun and made a calculated guess it was hollow. With a wink at my Undine, I knelt down and placed my hands on the damp grass and called upon Water as I would have if I weren't warlocked. I felt the ground tremble as red sparkles spread out from my hands and covered the ground in seconds. As I stood, I held my hands out to my sides and gently raised the sparkling net. With it came water. Lots of it. Held in the air by the net I'd woven from Arcane. Even when I was at my full height I continued to raise my arms as the water rose with it.

When I wavered, or lost strength, I touched Crwys's strength and knew he was preventing our friends from dying. In that moment, a single breath in time, I had removed all the water from the back yard and now as I brought my hands in close the net became a needle pointed funnel. I moved it over the black sun, drove it into the center and released the water. As it fell, so did I.

I watched as the black Arcane burst into millions of flecks of black and disintegrated in the night air. The water hit Circe like a falling piano and knocked her to the ground. Everyone took in deep breaths as the water washed over the Circle in a wave. I shivered on the ground as the cold water turned the dirt around me to mud and I clutched my arms around me.

The wolves, Levi and Ivan ran forward to the pregnant girl as Crwys came to me and took me in his arms. His warmth—Sweet Lady I'd never been so appreciative of his warmth before. He kissed my forehead and my cheek as I tucked myself into him as tightly as I could.

I sensed Bastien coming to us through the link and watched as he blurred and became the tall, broad, handsome LeBlanc I knew. "*Chérie*, we need your help. The knife…" he glanced back at the Circle. "Marilla is fading. I'm afraid we're going to lose them both."

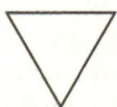

TWENTY SIX

"Shit," Crwys moved with me in his arms toward the Circle as the wolves stepped back, their heads bowed. Crwys put me back on my feet before he and Levi knelt down beside Marilla. The water had washed most of the blood away but it was obvious Circe had struck into the girl's belly.

Grey came up beside me. Even her wet, damp fur felt warm. "Crwys, did she hit the baby?"

"I don't think so, but Marilla's lost a lot of blood. Bastien, can you hear her?"

"*Oui*. But she is very faint. We can't hear the child."

I looked from Crwys to Bastien. "Is…is that bad?"

"It can be for a wolf." Crwys and Levi stared at one another, but didn't speak. When I got a good look at Levi's face, his eyes were black and his face…different. His demon was in control and they were communicating a different way.

Crwys looked up at the circle of wolves. "I need all of you to concentrate on her through your link. Keep Marilla here," then he looked at me. "Come here and put your hand on Marilla's side. I need you to find the baby in the link."

"Me?" I knelt down and Grey knelt down beside me. "But I don't—"

"Use the Arcane to find her. We need her to stay. Help her find her way back."

"Arcane? Crwys, I can't use that. It's just destructive power. I'll end up doing something awful—" Images of the house imploding and Fred disappearing came to mind.

Crwys put his hand on my shoulder. "Witches fear Arcane

because of its power, because it can and will destroy you if you let it. You control it. It does not control you. You have your Undine—she's there on your shoulder. You have me. You control the power," he moved his hand to my cheek. "I can't do this for you, babe."

I blushed. I was shaking, blushing and feeling all kinds of confused. But his pep talk worked and I could feel the fear and the anxiety in the link when I pulled the door open. "Crwys…do you know what you're doing?"

"Delivering a baby?" He gave me his best smirky grin and his eyes were solid red. "I've delivered more babies than a hundred of your lifetimes. Just keep her with us."

I closed my eyes and put my hand against the side of Marilla's belly. And then I fully opened the link's door.

I gasped at the cold I felt when I stepped through. And the darkness. I was in a wild wood, with blinking red and green eyes peering at me from the trees. Fear moved up my back like the whispering touch of spider legs. I wrapped my arms around myself as I took a few steps in the overgrown grass. Twigs snapped beneath my weight and I cleared my throat. "Hello?"

My voice echoed in the darkness and I felt kind of silly, though I felt the presence of dozens of minds. "Hello? Are you there?"

Something stirred in the brush to my right, beside a tree with roots extending above the ground. I saw something move, something white and small. With my first spark of hope, I moved toward it and had the impression it was hiding behind one of those roots. "Hello? It's okay. I'm not here to hurt you. Your mommy's very sick and you need to come out so you can see her."

I had no idea where these words came from, but they felt right. I looked to my right to see the faint outline of my Undine as she swam through the air and pointed behind the root. Nodding, I moved carefully and sat down on my side of the root. The tree was cold against my back and I was pretty sure my ass was wet from the damp ground.

"It's okay." I held out my hand on the edge of the root. "You can sniff me. I promise I won't chase you or hurt you. But I need you to trust me so you can see your mommy."

I waited. Watched the space above my hand. I heard rustling and thought I saw…

Sweet Lord and Lady of all things precious in this world.

The face of a tiny wolf pup with the whitest fur peered over the side of the root. She wasn't beside my hand, but a hands span away.

She looked at me with fearful but curious dark eyes. I smiled at her and leaned my head to my right shoulder. "Hello, beautiful. Go ahead and sniff. You can even bite."

When I said that, I didn't think she would. But as soon as she could, the little pup disappeared and reappeared at my hand. She sank tiny teeth into my finger and I held my tongue. When she let go there wasn't a mark on me. No blood, and abruptly no pain. "Are you satisfied, little one?"

The pup stumbled over the root and landed on her butt before she righted herself and came to my leg. I carefully moved my hand and offered it to her again. And this time she made a little noise that was kind of like a baby squeak before she tumbled into my lap. I rubbed her soft fur and made cooing noises at her as she gnawed on my fingers. And when I sat back, she climbed into my arms and rested her head at my neck.

"Sam?"

I laughed as she licked me and squeezed her tight.

"Sam? You can let go now."

The shrill cry of a baby snapped me out of the dream, or place or wherever I'd just been. I looked around for the pup but she wasn't there.

You bonded quite nicely. She thinks you're her grandmother, Grey said.

"Say what?"

Grey stuck her snout in my side. *Look at Crwys.*

I did, and my heart, like the Grinch's, grew about twenty sizes. He knelt on the wet, stone Circle without his jacket, because he'd bundled a tiny little pale baby inside of it. I put my fingers to my lips as he turned a bright face to me and smiled. He really, really smiled. "You did it! She's here!"

Yes, she was. But I turned and looked at Marilla, whose eyes had been closed. The mother had passed. Too much blood loss was my guess. But the child...

<Samantha! Thank you! Ma petite! Thank you!> Voice upon voice crowded in my head as the wolves crowded around to get a look at the little pale perigee

Wait...

I touched my face. Straightened my back.

"What is it?" Ivan said from where he stood behind Levi.

"I don't have a fever anymore. On no! Bastien!" I turned to him where he knelt beside Crwys. "The antidote."

"You have it," he said before he looked at me. "Our littlest gave it to you."

Huh?

"When she bit you, she released you. But you will hear us for some time as long as the pack wants you there."

Oh great. I'm going to have pack voices in my head. As if it wasn't already crowded enough in there as it was.

"Look out!"

The warning came through the link and in the open as someone shouted. We all turned in the direction of the voice to see Circe on her feet, the long knife raised above her head.

My ears popped and I swallowed. Everyone else waited for Circe to move, but she didn't. She looked like a tall, weird statue about to strike. A few wolves whined and lowered their heads and flattened their ears.

"I'm afraid that's not going to happen, dear Olivia," Cromwell Dryden's voice rang out above everyone.

I stood and turned to see him and the Clerics walking from the house out to the Circle. Of course, the ear popping. They'd set up a cap. If the mounds of turned earth bothered their progress, it wasn't evident. But what made me very nervous was there were still four Clerics and I knew Fred wasn't among them.

Cromwell paused in front of me and was careful to give Marilla's still body a good berth. He put his hand on my shoulder, smiled and squeezed.

Cromwell...smiled? I didn't know his face could do that!

He moved on to Olivia as the wolves parted. She was frozen in place but her eyes moved, following him. And I saw some serious hatred in those eyes. Cromwell put his hand on her shoulder as well. "Olivia Graham, magical name Circe, it is by the order of the Magical Parliament that I hereby arrest you for crimes against the faith, against the God Mother and against the Order of Ceremonial Magicians. I'm afraid Blackwood wants you incarcerated as much as I do."

One of the hooded and robed Clerics threaded their way around the Circle to Ivan. I was about to say something when she threw her robe back to reveal she was Miss Water. She abruptly wrapped her arms around Ivan's neck before the two started a deep and embarrassing kiss. My jaw dropped.

"I guess we know who he's been seeing," came Crwys's voice in my ear. He was still holding the baby and bouncing her up and down. I looked into her face and she opened her eyes.

I knew this was the little pup in the forest. I also knew she was forever a part of my life.

Great. I had a perigee for an adopted niece.

Bastien moved in on Crwys and took the baby. My boyfriend stood to the side as the wolves crowded in and they idly walked away toward the house. I thought I heard Bastien cooing at the baby and shook my head. Several wolves that had shifted back to their human forms lifted Marilla's body and carried it with them.

Ivan, Miss Water, Levi, Grey and myself stood in the Circle and watched as three of the robed Clerics clamped irons on Circe and led her away. I wondered if those irons they used would stop her from using her Arcane Magic.

Cromwell stepped up and clasped his hands in front of him. "I would at this time, like to thank the detectives for their involvement in catching Circe. Given your knowledge and," he looked at Levi. "Your own secrets, I can be assured you will keep this particular incident quiet?"

"Always," Levi said.

Crwys smiled. "Maybe."

Cromwell looked a little uncomfortable. "Maybe?"

"You going to lift Sam's warlock?"

"Detective—"

"I'm just saying, Mr. Dryden, that you have most of what you want. No you don't have your magic scroll, but you have Circe and you have the Hammer. Release Sam."

"Please," Miss Water said as she stepped into the conversation. "You saw how well she worked with her Undine, even while warlocked—"

"Dharma," Cromwell said with a hand raised. "We'll talk later about your part in all this, and about your new boyfriend. But for now," his gaze came back to Crwys. "The Codex was the bargain."

"Lift it, or I will ask for a Tribunal." I narrowed my eyes at Cromwell.

His smile sort of faded. "We'll be in touch," he motioned for the others to follow.

Dharma came up to me and looked sort of lost. "I couldn't stop her. She missed you so much, and with me getting to know Ivan," she glanced back at him. "She belongs with you."

"It's okay. And thanks. Was that you that told me to bring the water out of my sink."

"Yes."

"How did you know I had water in my sink?"

"Because when I asked her where she was, that's what she told me."

I looked at the retreating backs of the Clerics. "Where's Fred?"

Dharma shrugged. "I don't know and I don't care. Cromwell fired him yesterday, so good riddance. But...I gotta go. And don't worry." She patted my arm, gave Ivan a kiss and ran off to catch up with her Hive.

I immediately rounded on Ivan. "Does she know—"

"No," he put up his hands. "She knows what Arden knows. That I'm a good hacker and my Dianic Gift makes it possible for electronics to work around magic. That's it."

I narrowed my eyes at him.

Crwys grabbed my hand and pulled me to the house. "Come on. Let's go check on Jack and Kyle and then get the hell out of here."

I really liked that idea. "To where?"

He smiled. "Levi's..." And then he laughed as we hurried inside.

"Wait...what?" Levi said as he caught up to us.

TWENTY SEVEN

February 14th.

The decision to release the warlock didn't come until February the fourteenth of all days. For the removal I was called into the Cleric Office, which to my surprise was a large church on the way north out of the city. I'd recovered from the venom, had my equilibrium back and sort of had my confidence back as well.

No one had asked anything about Fred, which was a relief. Or about Arwen, which was also a relief, though I couldn't stop the guilt I felt for both of them. The Parliament didn't bring up my dad's house or the whereabouts of my dad either, and I had to wonder if that was because they were saving that for later or because whatever magic made the neighborhood forget had finally made them forget as well.

Ina's house was a disaster. Broken doors, smashed windows and a torn up back garden. I just wanted to bulldoze the whole thing down, but Crwys hired people to rebuild it. Suggested I put it on the market since the bodies that had been buried under the garden were no longer there. But I couldn't in good faith ever recommend anyone ever living there.

And besides, as far as the world knew, Inamorata Devonshire was still alive and off on vacation somewhere. As long as the mortgage payments were made and the utilities paid, no one cared.

As for Arden? She'd been elected as High Witch, just like she always wanted. I wondered if it was because of one of those things she stole from Circe's house.

Crwys, Ivan, Kyle and Jack met me on the front steps of the church as I walked out. They cheered and I bowed.

"How does it feel?" Ivan asked me. "To be un-warlocked." He frowned. "Is that a word?"

"It feels like I'm whole again." My Salamander appeared in the air over my right hand and danced. Once he disappeared, we piled into Ivan's Mini-Cooper and headed out for lunch. Crwys bowed out when he got a call from Levi about a body. We dropped him off at the station and he pulled me out of the car for a long kiss and embrace. We had become inseparable since the incident with the wolves and Circe. I spent several nights over at Levi's, where Crwys lived most of the time because his own place was, in Levi's own words, a dump.

And he'd spent a lot of time at my place.

I hadn't heard from Bastien or the pack in a week and I figured they were busy taking care of Regine, as Bastien so happily named her. I couldn't wait till she grew up and changed it.

Things had been quiet. Just the way I liked them.

"See you tonight," Crwys said as he pulled his lips from mine. "I'll probably be coming in hot." Which for him meant he'd be coming in from work.

"That's fine. I'll be there." I combed his hair back with my fingers. "And my Valentine's Day present?"

"I already told you yes," he winked. "I'll tell you who and what I am. I promise. You've been patient with me and it means a lot for you to know all of me."

"Interesting you picked one of the most expensive restaurants in the city to reveal this to me. You think I won't make a scene?"

"I don't think you'll make a scene anywhere," he kissed me again and then ran inside.

"You two are so cute together," Kyle said from the front as I slipped into the back.

I stuck my tongue out at him and patted my tummy. "Me and my Elementals are starving. Let us eat!"

* * *

The dinner reservation was at eight. By nine I was worried. And by eleven when the restaurant needed to close, I was livid. I paid for the food I did eat and heard my credit card scream at the price of crab claws. I'd dressed up in the clothing I'd gotten from Arden back in January and my hair was so shiny it was nearly blue under the restaurant lights.

Outside, I dialed Crwys's number for the fiftieth time. This time it went straight to voicemail and I was too pissed off to leave a message.

I turned toward the lot where I'd parked my Jeep and dialed Levi's number. I made sure I had it these days.

"Hey Sam," Levi sounded cautious. "Did he tell you?"

"He never showed."

Levi paused. "Oh. Really?"

"Yeah. And you already ruined the excuse he forgot." I sighed as I neared my Jeep. "He ditched me, didn't he? He never intended on telling what he is. Who he is."

"Man, Sam, I don't know. He was nervous about telling you. And I wasn't exactly that happy about him doing it."

"Because you think it makes him vulnerable."

"Yeah." I could hear him talking to someone. "Look, I need to go. Got a date myself. I'm sure he'll turn up."

I looked around at the parking lot. Watched a couple laughing and kissing in the corner under a magnolia tree. In fact, there were couples everywhere, walking, laughing, talking and kissing.

I seemed to be the only one alone.

"Sam?"

"Levi, if he calls you, tell him not to bother coming by the shop. We're done."

"Sam—"

"And I'll pay him back for what he's put into the place." My eyes burned as I blinked back raw emotion. It was hard to keep it out of my voice. "Just...tell him to fuck off." I disconnected, fumbled with the keys to my Jeep, got inside, and let the dam burst.

With all the terrible, crazy, horrible things in my life, Crwys had been the one bright, burning light leading me to peace. I somehow felt he was gone. Knew it somehow when he no longer tickled the edge of my mind. My Sylph appeared in the air in front of me. They no longer needed me to Call them. They were a part of my life again.

The Sylph looked sad as he hung his head and zoomed toward me to hug my face. I felt his love, his warmth and his attempt to make me feel better. All of my Elementals appeared in the car and comforted me. My Undine rested on my shoulder, my Gnome in my lap, her weapon tucked away, and my Salamander moved to sit on my head and look down over my eyebrows as his small hand patted my forehead.

I could feel their empathy, their need to help. They were trying to cheer me up. I had them back and I felt touched again by the God Mother. The Arcane was silent. And I was alone.

Again.

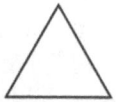

ELEMENTAL FLAME
CHAPTER ONE

February 14th, Two Days Ago

"Holliard."

"Detective, it's Arden Vervain."

Crwys held his breath for a full half minute as he toned down everything he wanted to say to the newly-elected High Witch of New Orleans. Counting down from ten never worked for him. Mostly because he just came up with ten insulting things he wanted to say. Especially to Miss Vervain. He made a mental note to get a new cell number. He planted a smile on his face as he looked at Levi, whose desk faced his own. His partner glanced up, frowned and tilted his head, then went back to his computer to finish paperwork.

"What do you want?" Well, the tone was brisk but he did sincerely want to know why this Witch was calling him. Things had been so quiet since their brush with the Magician Circe. He and Levi had collared three murder suspects and his relationship with Samantha Hawthorne had reached the place where he felt she needed to know what he was.

And who he was.

"Look, Holliard. We need to take whatever this is between us and set it aside. I'm calling you because the Obsidian Queen's contacted me about her price. She wants Sam and one of her Fetches managed to bring Sam to the clearing."

"What?" He sat forward. "What clearing?"

"The one on my property. The same place I made the deal with

169

her. I need you to get out here and stop this before she takes Sam with her."

"I'm on my way." Crwys jumped out of his chair, which rolled backwards as he jerked his leather jacket off the back. "I'm heading out."

"Was that Sam?" Levi asked as he pushed back from the desk.

Crwys slipped the jacket on and held up his hand. "No. Just… something I need to take care of." Normally, he'd bring Levi along with him. The two had been inseparable since the day their hosts met. Crwys was also aware of Levi's disapproval of his relationship with Sam. Levi had been there when Crwys fell in love for the first time, and he'd been there when his heart cracked at her loss. Levi also knew about the secrets that came from that pairing—secrets that needed to remain secret.

Falling for a human again was dangerous for Crwys, not just physically, but it could make him vulnerable in many ways. Taking care of Sam's problems shouldn't be set on Levi's shoulders so heading out to stop a Faerie Queen seemed like another day in Crwys's life. He would prevent Brendi from taking Sam and put an end to this. Brendi's father had asked for amnesty for Sam. The idea Brendi would go through a second party to get around her promise to her father—knowing a promise from a Faerie bound them to that promise—was atrocious. This could be the catalyst to oust Brendi once and for all.

"Don't forget your dinner with Sam," Levi called out as Crwys headed to the door. "And don't forget the roses!"

Crwys grinned. He'd bought a dozen roses and had them in a gold box in the break room fridge. He'd paid double what roses cost just because it was Valentine's Day, but Sam was worth it. She was worth a million times that amount. He grabbed the box out of the fridge on the way out and put them in the back seat of his '64 Mustang Fastback.

He dialed Sam's number as he got in and turned the key. The rumble of the V8 always boosted his confidence. The raw power of it reminded him of his youth, of days spent in the sun, in the wind, in utter ignorance of what his life would become.

When it went to voicemail he disconnected. No need to leave one if she was in that Circle. He cheated and put his portable light on the dashboard as he sped out of town toward Gypsy Gardens.

The dashboard clock read five twenty-two as he pulled into the long dirt drive leading up to Arden's house. He didn't see Sam's Jeep and wondered if she'd parked somewhere else on the property. He tossed his badge into the passenger seat but kept his weapon tucked into the back of his jeans as he got out of the Mustang and slammed the door.

A young woman came running out of the house, dressed in a ritual robe, waving at him. "Detective Holliard!"

"Hey," he said as she nearly barreled into him. He gently grabbed her upper arms to steady her. "Calm down and breathe. Where's Sam?"

"In the Circle!" The young girl pointed back to the house. "Just follow the path. My Lady's already there."

He assumed My Lady was the title the young Witch used for Arden. She was the High Priestess of her coven so it made sense.

Crwys took off toward the house at a fast run. The open front door was convenient as he made his way through the rest of the house to the back sliding glass doors and down an obvious path through the woods. He could sense power ahead and he could sense an open door.

Dammit!

He burst out of the forest into a clearing illuminated by torches and thousands of fireflies. Though a second look revealed these weren't actual fireflies, but pixies. Pixies!

The Circle was lined with robed people and he assumed they were Arden's coven. The light in this part of the swamp was dim because of the thick canopy of tree foliage overhead. He stopped just outside of the Circle, seeing and hearing the spin of the energy the Witches consecrated sphere. He could easily step through but he was also cautious as he moved closer to see inside. He needed to find Sam first and focus on her.

Two of the robed figures stepped aside as Arden stepped up to the edge. She was dressed in her usual black robe and silver jewelry. She produced a long knife and cut straight into the spinning energy. Everything paused as she slipped her hand inside and parted a door. "Quickly!"

His ears popped as Crwys stepped hurriedly through Circle door. He spotted the balefire in the center, Arden to his right, the hidden, robbed coven members surrounding him and the tall oval mirror to the right, the door into *Alfheim*.

He took a single step forward with the intent of looking behind the mirror to see if Sam was possibly behind it and realized his foot didn't hit the ground. Crwys looked down to see a thick, white mist covering the grass.

Alarms went off in his head as he realized Sam wasn't there.

Sam wasn't even on the grounds. And the only reason there would be mist between his feet and the ground would be to prevent any Faeries present from touching the Earth.

Something struck his chest with enough force to knock him onto his back. In his mind he went for his power, his core, the legend that made him what he was and released his primordial fire. But in reality, he couldn't move as he lay staring up at the pixies as they twinkled among the canopy of cypress, willows and alders.

Something obscured his vision, blurred in front of him. He fought to raise his right hand and touch the long, golden shaft protruding from his chest. His fingers moved along the smooth surface to where it met his flesh, the point buried in his chest.

He knew the arrowhead had found his heart. It was the only weakness he had. And someone had used the Arrow of Artemis to pierce it. He wrapped his hand around it and began what he knew would be a long, arduous process of tearing it out.

Strong hands took his wrist and pulled his hand away. He heard the clink and rattle of chains and shifted his gaze to look into the face of Brendi, the Faerie Queen of the Obsidian Court. He saw the bow in her hand and the quiver at her back.

"Bind him the way we you were told," she said to the robbed figures as their hoods folded back.

Crwys saw they were Faerie soldiers, not Arwen's coven, their silver moonlight armor hidden under the black material. He fought, or tried to fight, but there were too many of them as they turned him on his side and bound his wrists behind him, pulling his arms together tight. His thighs and ankles were equally cinched tight as he fought the desire to succumb to the magic of the Arrow.

"Do you have to do that to him?"

Crwys recognized Arden's voice through the haze. The soldiers lifted him up and held him under his shoulders. He couldn't stand and he couldn't fall as the pain of the Arrow in his heart seeped along his limps, paralyzing his power.

He kept his head up if not leaned to his left shoulder as he watched Arden step up to Brendi. Rage filled Arden's expression and he understood too well what Brendi wanted.

She wanted him.

The Obsidian Queen glanced at Arden. "Blackwood's information was accurate. You should be happy I chose him and not you."

"You promised to tell me why him," Arden pointed at Crwys. "What's so special about him?"

Brendi's expression softened. "Poor Arden. You've lived among Gods and never knew it. This man, this creature, is wanted in our realm, for crimes against our world. For lighting a fire that nearly destroyed us." She took several steps toward Crwys and put her fingers under his chin. He narrowed his eyes at her, willing her on fire.

Nothing happened. The Arrow did the job it was designed to do. Nullify him. Weaken him. Make him easy to handle. After all, that's what his sister commissioned it for.

"And you, Crwys Holliard. I have your name now. I know what you are, and who you are and a deal within a deal is always the best reward. And because I have you, I will have the hearts and minds of the survivors of our entire realm. Once they know I have the Destroyer, no one will oppose me." She leaned in and he could see her now inhuman beauty. There was nothing human left inside of her. Her pale, smooth skin, her long pointed ears, her catlike pupils and her sharp, pointed teeth.

She pressed a kiss of cold lips against his before she bit into them. He made a noise because he couldn't speak, and tasted his own blood. Brendi pulled back and smiled. He saw his blood run over her bottom lip and down her pointed chin. "Take him to the palace."

The soldiers holding him lifted him higher as they prepared to drag him through the mirror. One of the soldiers in gold armor reached out to grab the Arrow. Brendi drew a sword from a scabbard at her hip and sliced off his hand. The soldier cried out and went down on his knees as pure Faerie blood poured into the mist. "Never touch the Arrow! It cannot be removed. Do I make myself clear?"

The soldiers responded, "Yes my Queen!"

Crwys looked over at Arden as he was dragged toward the mirror. His eyes narrowed he summoned the last of his power, what little was left to him and cursed Arden Vervain. A single ember from the balefire shot into the air, spiraled down and burrowed into her heart. She cried out and clasped her hands to her chest as she stared at him, wide eyed.

She *knew* what he'd done. She knew he'd cursed her.

"Please! Don't do this! She gave me no choice!"

Her cries for her own salvation vanished as he passed into *Alfheim*.

Crwys moved in and out of consciousness as his body was dragged, dropped and then placed on an ice-cold surface. He passed into dark bliss, away from the pain of the Arrow for a time. But when he was awakened, he lifted his head and realized just how dire his predicament was as shattering pain followed him into wakefulness.

He recognized the Obsidian palace by its dark marbled interior and its cold, dead power. He also recognized the throne room where he hung suspended from chains that pierced his body. The chains ripped through his flesh and muscle and fused to his bones not only at his shoulders, but at every joint above his waist. They held his arms out from his sides as blood dripped into a bottomless pit below. The Arrow protruded from his chest, locking him into this body. He was crucified on the altar of the Obsidian Queen.

More chains encased his legs from his thighs to his ankles. The added weight pulled at the chains holding him in the air. Constant, steady pain.

Crwys had known agony in his long life, but never anything as excruciating as this.

"Behold!" Brendi shouted out from her facing throne. "The Destroyer!"

His eyes opened again at the cheers that went up around him. He lifted his head to see thousands of Faerie as they crowded in to see their devil, to see the one that turned their fertile fields to dust.

"We want to see his true form!"

"Show us his form!"

"Show us!"

Crwys smiled as his gaze found Brendi's. What her people wanted, she could not do. Not with the Arrow inside his heart. Like this he was sealed in place, not alive or dead. But if the Arrow was removed, he swore, no he *vowed* he would lay waste to her and every living thing in the palace.

As the pain increased he fell back into madness. The old lunacy that became a comfort for centuries before he woke to a life among the humans. Crwys made a small sound at first that built in volume until the hall became silent and his laughter echoed off the walls.

You still don't have what you want, little Queen. And without proof of who I am, your subjects will doubt you. Remove the Arrow and I will destroy you and your people.

He knew she heard him as her own eyes blazed with anger.

His last thoughts before he fell into a blessed darkness were of Samantha.

I love you, Sam. I will always love you.

174

Look for the next book in Eldritch Files, Elemental Flame!

Thank you for purchasing and reading Elemental Moon. It would be greatly appreciated if you could take a moment and leave an honest review of this book within the guidelines of your favorite retailer.

If you want to be notified when Phaedra's next novel is released and get free stories and occasional other goodies, please sign up for her mailing list by going to her website at phaedraweldon dot com.

Your email address will never be shared and you can unsubscribe at any time.

Glossary

Pronunciations:
Crwys - *Cruise*
Medbh - *Mayv*
Sidhe - *Shee*
Dijin - *Gin*
Alfheim - *Alf-hime*
Circe - *Seer-See*

Language:
I am not an expert in Cajun or French, nor am I fluent. But I always had it in my head that while Vampires in New Orleans was a very well thought out trope, Werewolves in the Bayou was just as important. So this is my own blend of the two.

Pischouette Mal Pris - Little girl's in a bad situation
D'accord - Agreement
Chérie - Darling
Ma petite - My little one (feminine)
Frére - Brother
Soeur - Sister
Chiot - Pup
Loup de chiot - Wolf pup
Diable du feu - Fire devil
Trés bien, mon ami - Very well, my friend
Tayeau - Hound
Diable - Devil
Tayeau petite - Small hound, insult; small dog.
Trés belle - Very beautiful
Mon frére - My brother
Homme mort - Dead man.
Je regrette - I regret
Bonne nuit - Good night
Jai faim - I'm hungry
Mère - Mother

Definitions:

Magical Parliament - a grouping of 13 High Witches chosen from all over the world to regulate magic use and the teaching of magic so as to avoid revealing a Witch's presence to the Cowen world. There are more than 13 High Witches at any given time, but only 13 are chosen to serve in Parliament.

Demon Realms - worlds that exist outside and yet beside the Material Plane. Other names used for these realms are the Mental, Astral, Abysmal, Ethereal, Peripheral, and sometimes Alfheim.

Mother's Tracker - The Parliament once granted tracking rights to some Elder Witches, especially those with Elemental Gifts. The last Tracker to officially receive this right was Samantha's mother, Elizabeth Hawthorne. The right gave them the ability to see, hear, taste, and smell trails left behind by a named target. This is the magic Eliza used to track Dionysus and made it impossible for the Leviathan to escape Eliza's abilities.

Elemental Witch - A God Mother's child who possess all five of the Elemental Gifts; Earth, Air, Water, Fire and Spirit. The combination of the elements make the use of Spirit possible, though small instances can be achieved with little training. Elementals use their own energy to power their magic as they transmute the magic inherent in the Material Plane into power.

Dianic Witch - A God Mother's child who does not possess any of the Elemental Gifts. Dianics are given Gifts such as second sight, telekinesis, telepathy, aural visions, clairvoyance, and psychometry.

Elder Witch - A title given to any Witch possessing three Gifts, one usually required to be Elemental, who serves on the local counsels under a High Witch.

Magical Sight / Other Sight - the ability to see magic. All Witches possess this ability, but not all Cowens do. Those that can are usually slightly touched with a Dianic Gift.

Circle - Cutting the Circle is the Witch's ability to cut a circle into the Earth, thus creating sacred space for ritual.

Drawing Down the Moon - The ability of a Witch to join with the God Mother through Her blood in their veins. The phrase is also used by Dianic Witches when referring to creating sacred space.

Athame - Usually a black handled knife. The Witch's ceremonial knife. Represents the Witch's will.

Warlock - Often thought to be the term given to male witches. It's not. This is a state of banishment, when a Witch's connection to their magic is removed.

Hierarchy:

Cowens - Non Magical folk

Dianic Witches - God Mother's children possessing only Dianic gifts, such as telekinesis and psychometry.

Hedge Witch - God Mother's children whose Gifts contain an inherent, working knowledge of all of the Gaia's plants. They possess a very latent touch of all the Elements but not enough to wield them. They generate their magic through these combinations of herbs.

Elemental Witches - God Mother's children who possess all five of the Elemental Gifts.

Elder Witch - God Mother's children who possess at least one Elemental Gift but have dedicated themselves to their craft and their follow Witches for the betterment of all of the God Mother's children.

High Witch - A position voted upon; a position of leadership, and not one to take lightly. In order to be a high Witch, a God Mother's child must have at least two of the Elemental Gifts and one Dianic.

Cyber Witch - Still fairly unknown.

Author

Phaedra Weldon is a writer and mother of one. Born in Pensacola, Florida, Phaedra was raised in the lush, green southern tropic of Georgia. She grew up on southern ghost stories told while eating marshmallows around campfires, or on the back of pick-up trucks in the middle of cornfields on chilly October nights. Phaedra currently lives in the South with her daughter.

www.ingramcontent.com/pod-product-compliance
Lightning Source LLC
Chambersburg PA
CBHW021152130626
46554CB00005B/1785